A LOVE CURSED CHRISTMAS WISH

A GODS CURSED PREQUEL NOVEL

LEISL LEIGHTON

PERMIEN PRESS

Published by Leisl Leighton as Permien Press. For more information, email: leisl@leislleighton.com

Cover design – Leisl Leighton and Samantha Marshall

Editor – KI Romanis

eBook ISBN: 978-1-922836-35-9; Print ISBN: 978-1-922836-36-6

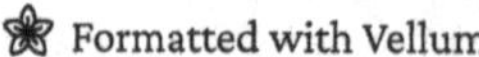 Formatted with Vellum

PRAISE FOR THE GODS CURSED SERIES

Was really hard to put this one down once I started! I can not wait to see what this new series ... Gods Cursed Series.... Holds in the future!

— **DIANA K – GOODREADS & BOOKSPROUT**

Loved this and it's Easter orientated. Check this out.

— **WHITNEY – GOODREADS AND BOOKSPROUT REVIEWER**

"So good! I will always love paranormal romances, they just have so many different types, and themes, and never get boring. Leighton delivers a great one!"

— **TAPNCHICA – GOODREADS AND BOOKSPROUT REVIEWER**

I absolutely love this ... Leighton brilliantly weaves in Greek and Nordic Mythology, and a HUGE splash of her rich and thrilling imagination. She is a master at world building, character, plot, and oh...those sex scenes are pretty damn hot. You'd be crazy not to read this series!

— **LAURA BADHUS – GOODREADS REVIEWER**

A LOVE CURSED CHRISTMAS WISH

CHAPTER

ONE

"Tam? Is that you? What are you doing here?"

Tam jerked around at the harsh whisper to see Bas standing in the darkened hallway – naked.

Ugh! He had to suppress his shudder even though this was not the way he wanted to see his father in the middle of the night. Unfortunately, he couldn't do the entire 'see no evil' thing any son would do if they saw their father's dangly bits because Bas had no idea he was a father. Tam's father. And he couldn't know. Not until Clodia's curse was lifted and the vow Eros had bound him with to keep him separate from the curse was no longer needed. If he told them before that, it would cause incredible pain – for all of them – and sweep him into the curse.

Clodia really had been evil.

As far as Bas was aware, Tam was a cupid who was helping a fellow cupid – partly out of the goodness of his heart and partly because he would gain some extra power by helping Bas end up with his fated mate.

Of course, the little matter of a love curse had to be

1

taken care of first, but they were a couple of months away from that being a possibility. If he could lay his hands on the old diary that had the information they needed to unbind the curse, then they had a chance. They would also need Jules Stevens to read it so she could start remembering her past lives – and her mate and the son of her soul – because she needed to be a part of the unbinding and neither he nor Bas could tell her anything about it.

Thankfully, he had a new lead on that old diary and hoped to have it soon.

But that wasn't why he was here tonight.

No, he was here because of the despair and hopelessness emanating from this house. As the years had passed, the curse had changed, deepened , becoming crueller than it had been. So he shouldn't have been surprised that it was now having this effect on his parents – that both of them were sinking into depression, losing all sense of hope in a better future. But he had been taken by surprise.

And now he was on the back foot because he needed to find some way of stopping what was happening with them and fast! Without hope, even if he found the diary and got Jules to read it, the curse would never be broken.

"Tamuel!"

He started. "What?"

Bas sighed. "I might not be able to see, but I know you're there. Don't try and pretend otherwise."

"I wasn't trying to pretend anything. I was just a bit shocked to see you down here. Like that." He flapped his hand at his father's naked body, even though he knew his father couldn't really see when in his human form – courtesy of the curse.

"You're the reason I didn't have time to put my clothes on. When I felt you here unexpectedly like this, I had to come down immediately." He shook his head. "Given you're so surprised to see me, that means you didn't come to see me. So why are you here? What's wrong?" Bas didn't even bother to try to cover his nakedness – and why would he from his perspective? Tam took after his father in many respects and those respects were something to be proud of – at least, Tam had always been quite proud of his endowments. And there was also the fact he was a cupid – they didn't suffer from false modesty the way many other Beings did. But still, this was a household with female witches and while one of them was Bas' mate, neither female knew that.

Tam opened his mouth to answer, but all that came out was a squeak as Bas took a step closer, moving further into the light.

Bas's eyes flared wide, the white that covered his irises making his sightless eyes glow in the darkness. "Did you find it? Have you brought it here?"

"What? No, no." Tam waved his hand as his father took another step closer to him, the light from the stairway behind him and the moonlight coming in through the windows beside the front door illuminating him even more brightly than he'd already been.

"Ugh," he said, putting his hand over his eyes. "Dude, put some clothes on, would you?"

Bas made a sound like a squelched laugh. "I didn't think you'd be a prude."

"I'm not. But you wouldn't like it if I suddenly appeared in front of you in my birthday suit."

"It wouldn't affect me at all if you did given right now you're a blur of colour and vibrational sound. I don't see details in my human form."

That was true but it wasn't exactly the point. "But what about when you're in your cat form? You can see then. You wouldn't like it if I paraded around in front of you in the altogether when you could see me during the day." Bas made a moue with his mouth as if he was about to disagree – of course he would. They were both cupid and it shouldn't be bothering Tam like it was.

Sighing to himself, Tam decided to change tack. "It's not me I'm worried about seeing you like that. What would Jules or Violetta say if they saw you wandering around the house like this? It would freak them out."

"You know Violetta helps nurse me after the shift from one form to another, so she is used to seeing me naked and thinks nothing of it. Besides she's not likely to be wandering around the house at this hour given she's just returned from a research trip. And if she did, it would freak her out more to see you here like this than it would to see me naked. Violetta doesn't take kindly to strangers suddenly appearing in her house."

"I'm not a stranger to Violetta, as you well know."

"She doesn't know you in this form, does she?"

"No, more's the pity. You know how hard it is to cover up this level of handsomeness all the time?" Tam shook his head and sighed. "But you don't have to worry about the whole stranger danger thing. I've made sure they can't see me on this visit."

"You're using magic to hide yourself and wandering around the house? That could hurt Jules!"

Tam raised his hand. "Hold your roll, son-of-Eros. This isn't a magic spell."

Bas raised his brow. "If it's not magic, then what is it?"

"Okay it is magic. But it's something that's not like the kind of magic that will upset Jules. I promise."

Bas narrowed his eyes at Tam – a curious expression for a demi-God who had been turned blind when he was in his humanoid form from sunset to sunrise from the curse he was under. "How do you know it won't hurt her. So far as I know, all magic has been able to hurt her."

"Well, this doesn't."

"I repeat, you know that how?"

"I've used it around her before."

"What? You experimented on her with unknown magic?"

"Of course I didn't. I didn't know she was there – she was supposed to be at a doctor's appointment. I was using it then so Violetta wouldn't sense me or my magic. I wanted to search through the library for something I'd heard was here. Jules just happened to walk down to the library while I was there. It wasn't like I could open a portal and leave while she was there, so I hid, hoping to Hells that she didn't have a reaction. And she didn't. Violetta didn't know I was there either. Not even when both of them walked right past where I was hiding in the stacks. The only one who seems to be able to see me is you. Probably something to do with the fact you can see auras when you don't have your usual sight. I wonder if—"

"Tam, stop rabbiting on about inconsequential things."

"The fact you can see me here isn't inconsequential."

"It is to me when I want to know how?"

"How what?"

"How are you doing it? I know it's not part of your power. I mean, you're a cupid, like me."

"Well, I'm not exactly like you. I have a different Mum and Dad from you with different powers from yours. My mum was a powerful witch like yours, but her powers were not healing ones, which makes my base-powers different. And secondly, I'm third generation cupid, not second like you. Eros is my grandfather, not my father."

Bas' eyes narrowed on him again as he folded his arms across his broad chest. "Still, the kind of power you're talking about ... it's not something any witch or demi-God should have."

"Well, I admit it's not my power."

"What?"

Tam shrugged. "I borrowed some power from someone who wants to help me out with this. They have the ability to change their outward appearance, even becoming invisible, kind of like a chameleon, but it's not magic as we know it. I have to drink their blood regularly for it to work and it only lasts for short periods." He screwed up his nose. "It's a bit yuck actually but needs must." He shuddered. "I'm not sure why people think vampires are sexy with the whole drinking blood thing because it's pretty disgusting, but whatever floats your boat."

"Tam," Bas said, his voice vibrating with impatience. "You're not dealing in blood magic are you?"

"Blood magic? Hells no. This isn't that. It's more a metamorphosis kind of deal with DNA and whatnot. While the blood is in me, it changes me enough so that I share in some of my friend's natural abilities. It's actually been pretty handy for other sneaky secret times as well as when I've needed to come into this house without Jules or Violetta being any the wiser." He held up his hand as Bas opened his mouth to answer questions, knowing he could see the gesture even if not the details of it. "Don't bother asking me who my friend is. Or why they're helping me. I can't tell you."

"Why not?"

"Like everything else, it's information you don't need. Information that could change how this – our little arrangement – needs to turn out."

Bas sighed. "Fine. But still, you shouldn't be here. You might not be using magic so as not to be seen, but you don't seem to be able to go long without using magic from what I've observed. And if you do it without knowing she's around, you could hurt Jules."

"I would never do that. It's why I entered through the portal I set up in the library." He gestured at the stairs behind him to cover the lie. He'd actually intended to come out of his portal in the library itself, but sometimes his magic didn't always work like it should and he'd come out of the portal at the top of the stairs. But Bas didn't need to know that.

He turned back just as Bas moved a step closer and further into the light that was coming through the windows on either side of the front door, illuminating the top of the steps that led down into the library where Tam still stood. Quickly, Tam looked back at the arch over the stairway. "Jules wouldn't feel the magic of the portal through all this stone and earth."

"She's getting more sensitive to magic," Bas said – Tam didn't even have to look at him to know he was frowning deeply. "I'm afraid very soon she won't even be able to stay in this house with the ley-lines connecting right under this house like they do and all the magic in the library and the Dangerous Books and Dark Magic room."

"There's shields and wards on that room though, right?" Tam said, turning back to face Bas and trying really hard not to look below his father's rather impressively broad chest.

Bas nodded. "Of course. But the way things are going, I'm not sure she's going to be able to handle any magic anywhere close to her, no matter how well shielded."

"Shit."

"Yes. Shit." He stared down at the marble floor, chest heaving. "I don't know what to do." His head lifted and his gaze collided with Tam's as if he could see him. "We have to make this work this Valentine's Eve. We have to. I'm not sure I could handle it if we don't. I'm not sure she could handle it."

Tam had to shove down the panic that rose up at the thought of what might happen to his mother and father if their plan to break the curse didn't work. He couldn't show Bas how truly concerned he was about both of them. So, instead of commenting on what his father had just said, he turned the conversation back to something he could handle.

"Bas, before this conversation goes any further, can you please put some pants on at least. I really didn't need to know Eros believed in circumcision for all his boys."

Bas huffed out a laugh – good. At least he wasn't so far gone he couldn't find his humour. But the humour died as quickly as it had come as he said seriously, "I'd have to run upstairs to get my pants. I'm afraid the small amount of magic I have access to can't even do something so simple as clothe me anymore."

Tam couldn't hide his gasp. "It's got that bad? Why didn't you tell me?"

Bas shrugged. "It's not something I talk about. And it had nothing to do with what we were planning. It's not like magic would help me do the research you needed me to do to help find the diary."

"Okay," Tam said, nodding slowly. "Well then, here, allow me." He waved his hand at his father.

Just in time. Bas took a step towards him moving fully into the light, but as he did, a pair of virulently green board shorts with equally bright pink flamingos all over them appeared on the demi-God. Bas looked down at them as if he could see them, rubbing his hands over the material. "You put me in board shorts?"

"I thought you could do with a little colour and fun."

Bas snorted. "Colour and fun? Hells. They're probably virulently pink or something, aren't they?"

"Maybe," Tam said slowly. "And green. They've got dancing flamingos on them."

"Zeus' Balls," Bas said, rubbing his head. "How are dancing flamingos on a virulently green background better than my naked form? They'll frighten the ghosts in the library."

"And your naked form wouldn't?"

"It might give them a thrill."

Tam chuckled. "Fair enough. But honestly though, why'd you come downstairs without a stitch of clothing on? Violetta might have seen you naked, but Jules hasn't. It's really not cool to walk around the house like that. You don't do that often, do you?" At least, he hoped not. He was going to have to pop in here more and more often over the next few months and he really didn't want to keep finding his father showing just how alike they were.

"Jules has seen it all before."

"Not in this life she hasn't."

Bas flinched. "You don't have to remind me of that."

"Sorry," Tam said, trying not to feel sick about how much pain the curse brought to his dad every day – more and more with every day that passed given the changes from man to cat and back again were getting harder on him. It was almost like the curse could feel they were getting close to breaking it and was punishing him for it.

Which maybe was why Jules was becoming more and more sensitive to magic.

And maybe it was why both she and Bas were losing hope.

He sighed and gestured to his father. "The pain ... is that why you're losing hope?"

"I'm not losing hope. Hope is all I have."

Tam stared at him hard. "Maybe that's true, but that in itself is a worry."

"Why?"

"It's sending you down a path of darkness."

"No it isn't. I'm fine. I'm just focused."

Tam sighed and shook his head. "Bas. I can feel it."

Bas glared at him for a long moment before he dropped his head, seeming to stare at the floor. "I know. I can feel it too." He raised his head. "But I'm keeping on top of it. You don't need to worry about me."

Tam chewed the inside of his cheek for a moment before nodding. "Okay. But what about Jules?"

"What about Jules? Jules is fine. I've been making sure she is fine."

"I'm sure you have but ..." He stared around him at the foyer. "Where's the Christmas decorations, Bas?"

Bas blinked and then glanced around at the joyless foyer as if he could see just how empty it was at a time of the year when it was usually overflowing with twinkling lights, wreaths winding up the stair railings and around the window and door frames. Different thematically coloured Christmas trees were usually set in each corner of the foyer and in each room. And there was all the Christmas-themed statuary, including nutcrackers and angels that usually filled up every single spare space along the walls and next to the doors. Not to mention the giant Santa with a motion sensor that made him nod his head and say 'Ho-ho-ho, Merry Christmas!' every time anyone passed.

There was usually also a soundtrack of Christmas Carols that played all day every day and enough bells and chimes hung around the place that, set off by any puff of breeze – including the air conditioning – created a tinkling musical sound day and night. The amount of light and sound that was usually in the foyer and the rest of the house night and day could not be missed or ignored, and yet it seemed Bas had not realised it was missing.

He blinked rapidly as he took in the total lack of sound and pine and cinnamon cents. "I-I …"

"Precisely. It's halfway through December and there's not one single indication that Jules' favourite holiday is coming. Why is that?"

"I don't know. She's been busy and … maybe she just hasn't felt like it yet."

"Has she finished her Christmas shopping?"

"Um—"

"Or even started it?"

"Um—"

"No? When her normal rule of thumb is to have all her Christmas shopping done before December even starts and all her Christmas decorations go up on December first without fail? If that's not a sign of despair and hopelessness, I don't know what is."

"Violetta hasn't been here to help her – she only got back today. You know Jules needs her grandmama's magic to help put the higher decorations up and do the lights on the outside of the house – after she leaves the house of course."

"That's an excuse and you know it. Even without Violetta here, she would have put up what she could manage. She finds joy in those garish decorations and twinkling lights, the carols and jingling bells as everyone in the vicinity of the house could attest to. But not only is she too full of hopelessness and despair to feel like putting them up, you are so full of those negative emotions, you didn't even notice she hadn't put them up. Which is not like either of you at all."

Bas' shoulders drooped. "You're right. I didn't notice."

"I guessed that." He sighed heavily and walked over to his father, hooking his arm through Bas' arm, turning him around to walk him towards the back of the house even though he knew his father did not need his help to navigate his way around the mansion.

The fact Bas didn't pull away or protest in any way said more than him not noticing the lack of Christmas decorations had. Bas never liked anyone treating him like he was an invalid. In fact, he reacted very badly to it any time anyone did.

Instead of punching Tam in the face though, he simply went along with Tam and only said, "But how did you notice? Have you been spying on us?"

Tam shook his head. "I didn't have to. I could feel it through the Realms. The despair and hopelessness that is building in this house is leaking out through the ley-lines."

"It is? But that is … how is that possible?"

Tam shrugged as he steered his father into the kitchen. "There is only one answer: Because you and Jules are more important to the Realms than we ever knew."

"I don't see how that's possible," Bas said as Tam pulled a chair out for him at the kitchen table.

"It's more than possible," he said as his father slumped into the chair. "It's apparently fact. Because if it wasn't, your negative emotions would not be affecting the ley-lines in the way they are."

Bas followed his movement as Tam went over and put

the kettle on. "I still don't understand why that brought you here. I mean, the only thing that can cure what's going on with us is to break the curse and we can't do that until Valentine's Eve."

Tam flicked on the gas under the kettle and turned back to face his father. "I hope that's not true because if it is, then we're in big trouble. In fact, all the Realms are in big trouble."

"What? How?"

"Because, if your negative emotions keep filtering into the ley-lines and out into this world and the other Realms, it will start to affect every living breathing Being it touches."

Bas stared at him for long moments. "Nonsense. Jules and I are not that powerful. Not that important."

"Given the fact I could feel your hopelessness and despair from the Realm I was visiting in my search for the diary, apparently you are. And I'm not the only one who thinks so."

"What do you mean?"

"There is another benefactor who is helping me. She pulled me to her palace and told me I had to come here right now to help you and Jules out of this slump."

"Why would a Goddess – I gather you're talking about a Goddess this time?" Tam nodded – he could share that much with his father – "Why would she care?"

"Because she can feel it too and it's beginning to affect her and all the other Gods and Goddesses in all the pantheons. Which means it's beginning to affect things here and in all the Realms. It's almost like the Eternal Well itself is weeping."

"That's ... that's not possible."

"It is more than possible. It's actually happening."

Bas stared at him for a long time. "What do you expect me to do about it?"

"You? I don't expect you to do anything right now other than to drink the tea I'm going to make for you and listen to my plan."

"You have a plan."

Tam smiled wildly as the kettle behind him began to whistle. "Of course. I came to help you and Jules find your Christmas cheer."

CHAPTER
TWO

"Bas!" Jules woke with a start, crying out for her friend as the nightmare images clung to her mind and body, making her feel like she was going to throw up. Normally he'd come racing across the room to her, even if he too was asleep and her terrified screams woke him abruptly from much needed rest. But tonight, he didn't come. She waited a moment but he didn't appear like he normally would to sit beside her on the bed, wrapping her in his comforting warmth.

"Bas?" she said, her voice raw. He still didn't answer. Didn't come to her side. She sat up shakily and looked around the room. It was empty.

Strange. Normally he didn't leave her until he had to go into his room before dawn so that he could change in the special containment unit Violetta had created for him so the magic of his change didn't set off Jules' magical allergy. She had never woken in the middle of the night to find him gone.

She began to shake, a sob rising in her throat.

He'd left her alone.

It shouldn't surprise her. She deserved it. Had been waiting for him to finally realise she was a soul suck and start to live his own life. As he should have long ago. She'd been trying to prepare herself for being truly alone for a while now. As a witch without any access to her powers and a magical allergy that was almost deadly to her and others around her, she had been alone in many ways all of her life.

Oh, she knew she was loved. Her grandmama loved her. And Bas loved her too, like a dear friend. But given Bas was a cursed witch who lived as a cat by day and a blind man by night, he had his own problems and she really needed to stop leaning on him like she did, expecting him to be her everything. It wasn't fair to him.

It was hard to let go though. He was her only friend.

A truly dear friend who put his needs and wishes aside for her.

Which proved just how much of a bad friend she was that she gave no true thought to his needs. Mostly. She *did* think of him. All the time actually. And she *had* encouraged him to do what he could to look after himself and do things that made him happy.

He always said being with her made him happy. And him saying that had made her happy so she had let him get away with it.

But she shouldn't have. She'd been weak. And tonight, finally, he must have realised how much she had taken from him.

Her grandmama, Violetta, had spent her life trying to find a cure for his curse, but of late she'd spent more and more of her time trying to find a way to cure Jules of her magical allergy. She hadn't completely given up trying to help Bas, of course, but since the death of Jules' parents when Violetta had become Jules' legal guardian, the attention she gave Bas' curse had become far less.

Which meant once again, Jules was ruining Bas' life.

It was no wonder why he'd given up on being with her twenty-four-seven tonight.

She'd felt this coming. Had felt the sadness in him rising over the last few months. He'd tried to hide the despair that had been building in him, but she'd sensed it alongside his growing fear that they would never find a cure to end his curse. She had to admit, it did seem hopeless. She wished it wasn't. Wished there was something she could do for him.

But she was useless. She had no power. No magic. And she collapsed in pain any time she came up against the slightest magic – if it was larger amounts of magic, she violently reacted to it in an explosive kind of way. Not that she exploded. The magic that touched her exploded in increasingly violent ways. The last time it had happened, Bas and Violetta had been hurt and a part of the library had been damaged.

She'd felt so horribly bad afterwards, particularly because she could do nothing to help heal either of them or put to rights what she had destroyed.

Tears flooded down her cheeks harder and faster and she couldn't stop them as her mind spiralled from that horrible day to centre on the thing she felt guilty about every day: not being there to support Bas when he went through his change twice a day. A change that had always been painful, but, despite the fact he was trying to hide it from her, she could tell it was becoming increasingly more painful for him. She'd heard his groans and moans as the sun rose in the morning and then again when it set at night. And she'd heard the worry in her grandmama's tone as she tended to him during and after. The time between him changing and then coming back to her side was getting increasingly longer as every day passed.

She pushed her knuckles into her eyes, trying to stop the tears. What right did she have to cry and feel sorry for herself when he was the one truly going through a bad time? A really bad time. A time that was getting worse. He never complained about it though, and if she tried to bring it up, he changed the subject, refusing to talk about it. If she pushed, he told her he didn't want to burden her with things that couldn't be changed.

She should have known what he truly meant was that he didn't want to share things she could never help him with.

And now, her best friend in all the world had realised just how useless she was, how much of a drain on him and everyone else she was, and he had left her.

Finally. As he should have done long ago.

Her breath shuddered out of her on a sob, and she wrapped her arms around her knees as she drew them to her chest, rocking back and forth as she tried to suppress the tears that threatened to take her over. She shouldn't cry. She had no right to cry. But ...

She was alone.

So alone.

She should just leave and disappear. If she took herself out of the equation then Violetta could give her full attention to curing someone who deserved to be cured. Who *could* be cured. Curses could be broken. Violetta had read about so many that had. There was hope for Bas.

For her though ... well, she was a lost cause. She wasn't under a curse. She was just quite simply a broken witch.

And it was time everyone realised it and gave up on her like she had given up on herself.

She hadn't even found any cheer in the fact Christmas was coming. Normally this was her favourite time of year, even though it wasn't a holiday witches usually got behind. They celebrated the pagan festival of Yule over a number of days as per the Luna calendar – days that always landed somewhere around December 25th. But while their celebrations were fun, and she did enjoy lighting the Yule log and hanging the pine wreaths and eating the Yule festival food, she had never been able to participate in the rituals as a proper witch should. It was too dangerous for her to go anywhere near them. Which was why Violetta had never been able to hold the festivities in this house since Jules was born as was her right as leader of the most powerful coven in the Southern Hemisphere.

It was another thing to feel guilty for. Especially given Violetta had allowed her to celebrate Christmas to keep up the tradition her parents had started for her.

They had given up on Yule because of her and had embraced Christmas festivities because the first time she'd gone out as a child and seen the decorations and the Christmas trees at the local shopping centre, she had been enchanted. It had lifted her spirits in a way nothing else ever had.

And after they were gone, she had thrown herself into the decorations and carols and gift buying-and-giving because it helped her to remember how much fun she'd always had with them, celebrating this holiday in a way that made it seem like it was theirs.

Except this year.

This year, the thought of Christmas brought no cheer. No uplift to her spirits. There was just a sense of growing sadness and loss. Everything was dull and lifeless and no amount of colour and lights, or pine and cinnamon scents, or the sound of Christmas Carols could lift her spirits. All she could see was a never ending repetition of day following day with no hope of true love or even friendships for her to cultivate.

Bas and Violetta were the only good things in her life. But now she was losing Bas and she had seen less and less of Violetta as her grandmama threw herself into trying to find a cure for Jules ... and for Bas when she had time.

She gripped her legs tighter and buried her head into her knees, pressing her thumbs into her eyes to try to stop the hot prick of tears that were creating an unbearable pressure in her head.

She tried to think of something positive, but it was hard, so hard, after waking from the horror of her nightmares once again only to find Bas missing and not there to comfort her as he usually would.

She wondered where he was. Was he downstairs doing his own research? Maybe she could go down and help him. She was good at research. It was her job after all.

She lifted her head. That was something positive to think about. Her research. It filled her days and made the interminable length of them bearable. While she researched every day, the research itself was different every day. She read about new things all the time. Learning and cataloguing information was her jam. It had always made life worth living.

Except ...

More and more recently, she was unable to help Violetta with at least half of the massive library because the grimoires and manuscripts held too much magic. Increasingly she'd been unable to catalogue the new boxes of books and grimoires that came to them from those coven members whose job it was to travel the world and find copies of all important works, as well as the more obscure works from unknown covens and magical Beings. She had always loved pouring over the new works that came to them, learning obscure pieces of lore and information. But more of what was arriving contained magic and while in the past she'd been able to deal with the pain a small amount of magic in the books and grimoires contained, now, the pain had become too much and she wasn't even able to be near the ones with the slightest amount of magic, let alone touch them.

Which pretty much meant she could never touch or look at any of the thousands of grimoires, books and scrolls they had in the library ever again. Even though some of them did not have magic bound into their pages, they had discovered that even if she read a spell, it could be disastrous for her. And for those around her. That was what had caused the latest magical allergy explosion a few months ago that had hurt Violetta and Bas and damaged so many of the stacks.

Not a good day.

In fact, it had been the start of her feeling like this.

The creep of it had been slow, and inexorable. She'd tried to lift herself out of it when she'd first felt it, but all her efforts had come to naught. She was falling into a depression.

Scratch that. She had already tumbled into the hole with the black dog and it was gnawing on her day and night and she couldn't escape it.

She wasn't even certain she wanted to escape it. Maybe giving in to it would be for the best. Maybe—

The door slammed open. She looked up blearily to see

Bas charge into the room. He was bare chested but wore an incredibly ugly pair of fluorescent green board shorts covered with violently pink dancing flamingos. She frowned as she took them in, not recognizing them as anything he'd ever worn before.

Her surprise at the board shorts only lasted for a moment as the sight of him, the fact of his presence, overwhelmed her with relief and the flood of tears burst through the damn once again. The sight of him blurred as she gave over to the need to cry.

"Jules," Bas said, running across to where she sat rocking and sobbing in her bed. "Jules, Jules. Don't, please don't." He reached her, sitting on the bed beside her, pulling her into his arms.

It felt so good. Far too good. But even though she knew she shouldn't – she should tell him to go and live his own life – she couldn't stop herself from clinging to him, to wanting to never let him go even though it would be the best thing for him.

Yes, she was *that* selfish.

The thought made her cry even harder, her words almost unintelligible as she sobbed into his shoulder. "Bas. Bas. You didn't leave me alone. You're here. You're here."

"Of course I'm here. I'd never leave you." One hand stroked her hair, the other holding her tighter to him just how she needed as his voice rumbled through his chest in a way that comforted her like nothing else could. "I had just got out of the shower when I thought I heard something downstairs. I went down to check, only for a few minutes. I didn't want to leave you alone. I didn't think you'd wake up while I was gone."

"I h-had a n-nightmare."

"I'm so sorry I wasn't here for you."

"It's o-okay. I-it's ok-kay. You sh-should be able t-to leave m-me," she blubbered. "I sh-shouldn't keep you to m-myself so s-selfishly. You h-have your o-own life to l-live."

He pulled back from her a little as if he wished to look down at her even though she knew he couldn't see her. He cupped her face in his large, warm hands. "No, no. My life is here with you. I always want to be here with you."

Her eyes starred with tears as she looked up at him, breathing in his scent, soaking in the warm comfort of her best friend. "I always w-want to be h-here with you," she said. But she was unable to continue with that thought. Pain clenched her stomach as the words left her mouth and she cried out, curling around the pain.

"Jules. Jules. What is it? What's going on?"

"It's the curse. It's getting worse," a disembodied voice said from somewhere over near the door. Were her tears that bad she could no longer see?

"No, no, this is no good. We don't have the time I thought we had," it continued to say. She didn't recognise the voice and still couldn't see who was speaking even though the voice moved closer. Not that she truly cared. It didn't matter. Nothing mattered. Not with this pain thrumming through her, and despair filling her like the heaviest meal she'd ever eaten.

"I c-can't ..." she began before sucking in a pained breath.

"Jules?"

She looked up at Bas, at his worried frown as his blind eyes tried to see, to figure out what was wrong. She hated that she worried him like this. Things were worse than she had imagined. She wished he'd never come back. "I c-can't ... I can't d-do this anym-more. C-can't be l-like this anymore. Th-there is no hope. N-no h-hope."

"Tam?" Bas said, looking behind him, panic in every line of his face and body.

"It's worse than I thought. We have to do something now."

"But what? What can we do?"

"Make a Christmas wish," the voice called Tam said. "It was what I was about to tell you before you took off suddenly to come up here."

"I had to come. I felt Jules cry out for me and her depression … it was so much worse."

"Which is exactly why we have to make a Christmas wish."

"A Christmas wish? How will that help?"

"I don't have time to explain it right now. It has to be good enough that I just know it will. And if we make it together, it will be all the stronger for it."

"But what should we wish for? What will cure her and me of this?"

"Let's wish for you both to find hope again. Enough to get you through this until it is time to break the curse."

Their words tumbled around her, making no sense. But then again, nothing made sense right now. All she was was pain and despair and hopelessness. It filled her. Covered her. Was turning everything grey. Threatening to turn everything black.

"Quick, hurry. Before she's too far gone."

"What do I do?" Bas shouted, his voice full of fear and panic.

"Hold my hand and say these words with me:

I wish this Christmas to find our joy
I wish this Christmas to find our hope
I wish this Christmas to feel our love

A LOVE CURSED CHRISTMAS WISH

I wish the Christmas spirit to fill us up
To get us through until we're cured
And everything is set to rights
The spirit of Christmas come to me
The spirit of Christmas come to her
The spirit of Christmas be in our hearts
The spirit of Christmas never to depart
All hail the spirit of Christmas."

THREE

Bas stared at the cupid in front of him, arms tightening around Jules as she sobbed harder against his chest. "You are not asking me to do a spell in front of Jules."

"No. Of course I'm not. Can you not tell it's not a spell? It doesn't even rhyme."

"Not all spells have to rhyme."

"True," Tamuel said. "But this isn't a spell, I promise. It's a wish. To the Spirit of Christmas."

"The Spirit of Christmas? How is sending a wish to the Spirit of Christmas going to help us? It's not like it's a God or anything? It's just a feeling."

Tamuel blinked at him for a moment. "Oh, the Spirit of Christmas is rather more than that. In fact, I think he'd be rather upset to hear you talk like that."

"He?"

"Of course, he. Are you telling me you don't know who I'm talking about?"

"Why would I know who you're talking about? Christmas wasn't even a thing when this curse was placed on me and I've been stuck with the Stevens wherever they've lived ever since."

"Yes. Which means you've lived in this house with Jules all these years with her celebrating Christmas. I assumed you, like her, believed."

"Believed in what?"

"Santa Claus. Who else?"

Bas snorted. "Santa Claus isn't real. Jules knows that too. She might have believed once upon a time, but she grew up."

Tam gestured at Jules. "Oh, she believes. Maybe not in the jolly man in the red suit that children believe in, but in the feeling he engenders within people. The Spirit of Christmas. It is personified in the person of Saint Nicholas aka Santa Claus. And he is very real, believe me. And rather partial to a good single malt scotch. I send him his favourite every year after Christmas is over."

"What?"

"Well, surely Santa Claus should get gifts too? And it doesn't hurt to stay on his good side. His spirit affects many things beyond just the Christmas season. Which is why it's so important to make the wish to him now. And it has to be as strong as it possibly can be for him to take note of it at this, his busiest time of year. If you want you and Jules to get through to Valentine's Eve, you need to do this."

"It can't be as simple as saying a wish out loud."

"It isn't. You have to believe."

Bas blinked at the cupid for long moments. "Believe? How can I suddenly believe in him to any great degree when I didn't even know he truly existed until a few moments ago?"

Tam shook his head. "It doesn't matter that you've only just found out. If you want this to work, you have to believe in the words we will say together. You have to believe they will get to Santa. And you have to believe that he will act on them and send the true essence of his Christmas Spirit this way to help us in this moment of our need."

"But ... How can my belief have any weight when Jules, the person who you say always believed, no longer seems capable of doing so?" She was sobbing so hard against him now, her tears running down his naked chest, the despair in them sinking into his skin. "Jules, Jules, it's okay. I'm here. I'm here. We're going to help you. Just hang on."

Rather than helping, his words seemed to make her cry harder and then all of a sudden, she became limp in his arms, as if she'd passed out.

"Jules! Jules! Tam what's happened? What's wrong with her?"

"Fuck. She's so far gone she's almost comatose. Bugger. I had hoped to get this done before she was this far gone. It would have been helpful if her usual belief was still at least a little intact. But given she's not capable of much of anything at the moment, we're going to have to do all the work for her. Do you think you can do it? If not for yourself, for Jules?"

Bas stroked her hair back from her face, wishing he could see her right now. He leaned down and kissed her forehead. "It's okay, Jules. We're going to help you. We're going to make this go away. Tell me exactly what I need to do?" he said, turning back to face where Tam stood while trying not to let fear overwhelm him. She didn't even seem to be interested in the fact he was talking to someone she couldn't see. Her depression and hopelessness was worse than even Tam had thought. Jules was never-endingly curious about everything. If she was her usual self, she would have immediately insisted to know whom he was talking to and what they were talking about. She'd want Tam to show himself. She'd want to know all the ins and outs of everything he was saying. Especially given he'd mentioned Santa Claus and that he was real.

She'd probably want to meet Santa.

But all she did was lie in his arms as if nothing in the world would ever interest her again. As if she'd already given up. As if she was already fading away from him.

His heart ached with his own hopelessness, but it got even heavier with hers added to it. She didn't know there was anything to hope for. And he couldn't tell her. It was something she had to find out for herself and she couldn't do that until they'd found the diary.

It was a bloody mess and this cupid thought it could all be solved by sending a wish to Santa Claus. It was crazy. Totally insane.

And yet, if it was the only way to help Jules, he'd just have to do it despite feeling the way he did. Taking in a shuddering breath, he said, "I can do it."

Tam tsked. "You need to sound a bit more enthusiastic than that."

"I can do it," he said more determinedly. "I *will* do it." His desperation to help Jules gave the sentiment weight.

Tam obviously felt it because he clapped him on the back and said, "That's the spirit. Now, hold my hands and repeat after me."

Bas laid Jules on the bed beside him – she didn't even whimper in protest, just lay there as limply as if she was asleep although he knew she wasn't – and then turned to take Tam's hands.

Tam repeated the wish, pausing after each sentence to allow Bas to say it too. Then once they were done, the younger cupid said, "Now we have to say it together. And when we do, we have to put every ounce of belief we have ever had in anything into it. We have to fill it with determination. We have to give it everything we've got. Can you do that?"

Bas nodded. Hopelessness might be filling him more and more every day with a growing certainty that his misery would never end but while he was struggling to believe there was any hope right now, the one thing he'd never lost faith in was Jules. He had faith that with a little help, she would draw on the strength he knew she had inside her and would get through the next few months. That she would be able to face continuing hardships and eventually win the day, breaking their curses and giving them back what was stolen so cruelly from them two thousand years ago.

"Ready?" Tam asked.

Bas nodded again and gripped Tam's hands more tightly. Then as if they'd practiced this over and over, he and Tam spoke perfectly in union, saying the words reverently, imbuing the words with all the belief he had inside him for Jules, for her love, for her strength, for her belief, that once returned to her, would see them through.

The sound of the words hung around them, echoing in the room, resonating in a way spoken words usually didn't unless creating a spell. But the air did not buzz with magic and there was nothing to indicate they were creating any kind of spell – as Tam had assured him – they were simply making a wish.

A wish to give Jules back her Christmas Spirit.

As the last sentence was said, the words appeared in the air around them, pulsing with a shining light of gold and green and red. He had no idea how he could see them with his sightless eyes, but he could. They must have sunk into the aether somehow and were imbued with a kind of astral aura. He watched, wide-eyed as they began to spin above their heads, brighter and brighter as they spun faster and faster. Then with a loud clap and a suck of wind that ruffled his hair, they disappeared.

The world around him fell dark again – except for Tamuel's aura in front of him and Jules' dimmed aura beside him.

"Now what?" he said after a long moment of silence.

"Now we wait to see if it worked."

"It might not have worked?"

Tam shrugged. "If we did it right, it should have, but I don't know."

"Can you not go to Santa Claus and ask him in person? I thought you said you knew him."

Tam snorted. "You need an invitation at any regular time if you want to visit the North Pole. There's a whole pass situation that allows you in but they don't give out those to just anyone. Particularly at this time of year. They don't want anything disturbing Santa in his duties. So even if I had one that allowed me in now, his elves would chase me out. And if they didn't, his reindeer sentry certainly would."

"Why? Because he's too busy getting ready for his epic sleigh ride to deliver all the presents?"

Tam laughed. "Of course not. That's just a myth. Santa doesn't deliver presents anymore. Parents do that."

"Then what does he do?"

"He is the embodiment of kindness and generosity. Of belief and everlasting hope. His job, his only real job, is to bring those things to the world within the Christmas Spirit."

"But why only at Christmas?"

"It's when he came into being, changing from human to something truly magical. It's when he is most powerful. And if he does it right, if he can imbue it in enough people, especially people like Jules who multiply it for him, then it can last in some form for the rest of the year. Which is why it's incredibly important that he not be turned from that job right now. Sending Christmas Spirit out into the world, especially with how cynical everyone has become and with all the strife going on consistently, it takes all his energy and concentration."

Bas frowned. "But won't our wish stop him from doing that?"

"No. Wishing to him at Christmas only makes him stronger, because it means we believe in him. And with that belief, he can do remarkable things."

"Like pull Jules out of this slump?"

"Yes. And you. You need to be pulled out of your slump too."

"I'm fine. My only concern is Jules."

Tam sat down on the bed beside him and put his hand on his shoulder. "You're anything but fine. Which is understandable. But Jules isn't the only important one here. And she will not be affected by the Christmas Spirit in the way we need her to be if you are still depressed and full of hopelessness. She is your mate, so what affects you affects her and vis-versa." He patted Bas' shoulder. "So this has to work for both of you or it won't work for either of you."

Bas sighed heavily. "I don't feel any different."

"We don't know if our wish has been heard or accepted yet."

"When will we know?"

"You'll know."

"How long will it take?"

"I don't know. A few minutes or a few hours. Maybe even days depending on the strength of our wish and what other wishes Santa is granting."

"Days! Jules can't continue to be like this for days!"

"I did tell you Santa is busy. And we're not the only one sending Christmas wishes to him. Every kid in the world who believes in him is sending wishes every day. Every time one sits on a proxy Santa's lap and tells him what they want for Christmas, a wish goes out to the real Santa Claus."

"Hells. That's a lot of wishes."

"It is. But I'm sure he will hear ours and do something about it. After all, the fate of the world depends on it."

Bas snorted. "I don't know if we're that important."

Tam's fingers tightened on his shoulder. "Believe me. You are."

Bas turned and climbed fully onto the bed, pulling Jules into his arms again, needing to feel her there in body if not in spirit. "So how will this work?"

"Don't know."

"You don't know?"

"Nope. Nobody ever does. The granting of wishes and how they're granted is completely up to Santa. I have no idea how he will interpret our wish or how he will decide to fix the problem."

"But I ... what if what he decides on doesn't work?"

"I have faith. As you need to do too. I know Jules would if she was able to right now."

"Okay." He had faith in Jules. Faith in the fact that her light would shine through the darkness. Faith that after all the years of loneliness, emotional torture and struggle, things would work out for both of them. It had to.

He stroked his hand over Jules' hair, filling himself with that faith; with that hope and belief. And as he did, something rushed through him. Something warm and good, full of empathy and kindness. His skin prickled with it, heat chasing over his skin.

In his arms, Jules shifted, murmuring something too soft for him to hear. Then, as bells tinkled in the air around him a 'Ho-ho-ho' that was deep and jolly rang through the room, making him smile.

Tam clapped his hands and jumped to his feet shouting, "Thank you, Santa."

"You're very welcome, my friend," the jolly, deep, echoing voice said.

The prickling warmth on Bas' skin began to increase, growing hotter, sinking in deeper until the warmth of it was in every part of him. He'd be worried it was magic except ... Jules wasn't reacting like she usually would to the presence of magic. There was no seizure or crying out as her body tightened with a rictus of pain – she said it felt like being slashed with a thousand cuts while being pummelled from the inside and out.

There seemed to be no pain now though. Instead she murmured again, stretching sinuously in his arms as if she too was being imbued with the warm joy tingling through his body.

"Oh-ho-ho, it's working," Tam said from where he stood beside the bed. "She's waking up. And she's smiling."

"She is?"

"She is."

Happiness began to bloom in Bas' heart.

Until the clock began to strike in the distance. Shit! Dawn was about to arrive. He had to leave this room, get away from Jules before the change took him over. He went to move, but her arms clamped around him and her voice, sensual and husky, said, "Where do you think you're going?"

She rose up in front of him, a sexy smile on her face and—

Holy Hells! He could see! He could see her beautiful face! And he was still in his human form.

How was this possible?

He glanced to where Tam had been standing, but the cupid was now at the door, waving at him. In his mind he heard, *"That Santa is just too clever. I'll leave you two alone for now. Enjoy. See you tomorrow."*

Then the younger cupid opened a portal and left.

Bas opened his mouth to shout out "No!", his arms going around Jules, ready to pull her off the other side of the bed to try to protect her from the magic as best he could, but before he could her lips landed on his in a kiss that stole the breath from his lungs, the sound from his voice box.

The magic hadn't affected her.

And she was kissing him like there was no tomorrow.

Maybe there wasn't.

For the life of him, suddenly he couldn't bring himself to care. All he cared about was the woman in his arms and the fact he was finally doing something he'd wanted to do with her for two thousand years.

He pulled her closer and kissed her back.

FOUR

Oh my! She was kissing Bas. The cursed man who had been living as part of her family for hundreds of years. Maybe even longer. Nobody could remember and he wouldn't – or couldn't – talk about it.

She was kissing the man who was her best friend. Her only friend. The person she cared for the most in the world aside from her grandmama.

She was kissing the man she loved.

Oh Goddess. She loved him!

When had that happened?

She couldn't quite remember exactly when, but it felt like a very long time. Longer than she'd even been alive.

She jerked as a thought hit her.

Oh!

It *was* longer than she'd been alive.

Whispers of memory that seemed to belong to someone else, yet also belonged to her, swam in her mind.

A past life? Yes. That's what it was. A past life in which

they'd been lovers though? It certainly felt like that was a possibility. It certainly felt like she knew this. Had shared kisses with Bas before.

Her Bas.

And he was. Her Bas. He had always been her Bas. Always would be her Bas. It didn't matter that she hadn't known that even a few moments ago. Didn't matter why she suddenly knew it now. All that mattered was that she did know it.

And that he was kissing her and she was kissing him back.

His tongue was in her mouth. Hers met his, sliding along it, twining with it, tasting it. Tasting his mouth.

Goddess he tasted good. Better than anything she'd ever tasted before. Orange and spice and all things nice. She giggled. He was like her favourite ginger Christmas cookies – except even better. If he was the last thing she ever tasted, she would die with a smile on her mouth.

Although, she didn't want to die. She wanted to experience this. More of this.

More.

Her hands ... Even though she'd been the one to instigate this, he'd taken over. When had he taken over? She'd been so lost in the wonder of sharing this kiss with him she hadn't cared, hadn't noticed and her hands had fallen back to her sides. But now she had to touch him. She lifted her hands to his chest, her fingers moved, curled into hard muscle.

He was bare chested. She was so glad he hadn't put a shirt on. He always wore clothes around her. Was actually quite careful that she never saw him without the barrier of clothes between them. And she had often longed to see what he wouldn't show her. Now, here he was, in her room, shirt off, tongue in her mouth, arms wrapped around her and ...

She dug her fingernails into the warm silken skin of his chest. His muscles flexed under her touch and he moaned, the sound a vibration in her mouth, against her fingers.

Oh Goddess. Her muscles clenched in her stomach, between her legs. Moisture flooded there too.

Wet.

She was so wet.

Bas was making her wet.

She moaned into his mouth.

His hands clenched against her back and he tipped his head and kissed her harder, deeper, faster, sucking her tongue into his mouth.

Goddess, she was going to pass out with the pleasure of it. Her mind swam wildly. If he wasn't holding her so tightly, she might have collapsed.

Not that that would have been such a bad thing – they were on the bed and it would be a soft land—

The bed! They were on the bed.

Kissing on the bed. Touching breast to chest, hip to hip, thigh to thigh and – she smiled into his mouth – erection to fully wet core.

She pushed her hands up his chest, raking her hands against all that warm, hard skin, all the way to his shoulders. Then she pushed.

He didn't budge. Didn't fall back as she wanted him to.

So she moved her hands again, up the strong column of his neck, over his jaw – ah, the roughness of his stubble against her fingertips, her palms ... delicious. Erotic. She wanted to explore it further, but what she wanted more was him. All of him. Inside her. Now.

She had waited so long for this. Too long for this. She hadn't known, hadn't realised just how much she had wanted him or how long she'd been wanting him. All her adult life.

Scratch that.

She'd wanted him for much longer. She'd wanted him for *all* her adult lives. Centuries. Thousands of years. Ever since ... ever since ...

Her stomach clenched – not in the way it had before, all tight and warm and tingly and pleasurable, but in a way that made her feel nauseated – and she stiffened.

He pulled back from kissing her, one hand moving up to cup her face while the other hand kept her pinned to him, hip to hip. "What is wrong," he whispered, breath coming hard and fast as he stared into her eyes as if he could see her.

"Nothing. Nothing. Kiss me again. I don't want you to stop."

He frowned down at her, eyes searching hers – could he see her? She rather thought he could. Although, why that was so strange, she didn't know. Couldn't remember. Not that it mattered. All that mattered was that he'd stopped.

"Are you sure?"

"That I want you to kiss me? That I don't want you to stop? Absolutely."

He smiled at her. That twitch of lips that made her want to grab him and lap the smile right from his beautiful, plump lips. How could a man have such wonderfully plump lips with the kind of definite bow to them that made her fingers itch to want to trace them, to follow the line that delineated the pink of his lips and the brown of his skin, skipping over to the little dent at the corner that popped out when he smiled just like he was smiling now.

The smile he only ever smiled when looking at her."

The fact he had a private smile for her made heat chase over her skin, sinking into her, flaming the fire inside her to greater heights. Hells. She was going to burst into flames if she didn't do something about this need inside her sooner rather than later.

But he was saying something to her. Something that was stopping him from kissing her. Nothing should stop him from kissing her. It was wrong. But he seemed intent on whatever it was and if it was important to him, then it was important to her. He also seemed to be looking at her in a way that said he expected a response – and that response wasn't for her to shove him back on the bed, rip off those ridiculous board shorts and ride him until she passed out with the pleasure of it.

Oh. Had it got hotter in here suddenly?

She lifted her hand from his jaw and wiped her brow. "Sorry, what were you saying? Your stubble was distracting me." His stubble and everything else about him.

That smile again. He really needed to stop smiling at her like that because she could barely concentrate on anything else when he did.

His lips were moving. Crap. He was repeating what he'd said and she was missing it once again. She put her hand over his lips – they felt so soft and warm against her finger-tips. "Sorry, I got distracted by the way you're smiling at me. Can you start over? And this time, I promise I'll concentrate."

His lips moved against her fingers – he was smiling again. She closed her eyes and lifted her fingers. "Ready."

"I was simply saying that I wasn't asking if you want to keep kissing me. I was asking if you were sure there was nothing wrong."

There *had* been something wrong. She remembered that feeling of panic and terror that had taken her over briefly, but for the life of her, she couldn't remember what had caused it.

But that didn't seem to matter right now. The only important thing as far as she could see was what was happening here, between them. The only thing of import was that she wanted him and he wanted her.

Because she loved him and wanted to show him how she felt with her body in a way she'd never shown anyone before.

Naughty, hot, sexy thoughts flashed through her mind ... oh, so many things she wanted to do to, and with, him to show him just how deep and forever her feelings for him went.

She cocked her brow at him and drawled, "Oh. No. There's nothing wrong. Well, there are perhaps two things wrong."

"What? Tell me."

"Well ... the first is," she said breathily, the sexiness of that husky sound like fingernails raking over his already hard as rock penis. He swallowed the hiss of breath that threatened to escape his mouth at the sound, because she'd opened her mouth to keep talking and he didn't want to miss it. "The first is ... that you stopped kissing me."

Bas was surprised his eyes didn't curl up into the back of his head as those words left her lips. The pleasure of them ... it was incredible. Almost as incredible as the reality of kissing her had been. He thought he'd remembered just how amazing kissing her had been, but the memory of the kisses he'd shared with her thousands of years ago was but a distant echo of the astonishing reality.

It was everything. It was breath. It was life. And he

never wanted to do without it again. Wasn't sure why he got to do it now. Unless it had something to do with his and Tam's insane wish being granted by Santa, the Spirit of Christmas.

It had to be that.

If he'd known about this Christmas wish thing years ago, he could have saved all of them a lot of grief! But that was a thought for another time because Jules – his Jules – moved a little closer to him, wriggling a little against his incredibly hard cock. He moaned – he seemed to be doing a lot of that – and did his own wriggling against her, making her moan in return.

By the Gods, he loved that sound as it vibrated in her throat and erupted out of her mouth. He wanted to put his hand on her throat to feel it, the other one on her chest to feel it there too. But before he could do just that – before he could cup her breast and delight in the weight of it and the hard point of her nipples against his hot and needy hands – she moved her hands up into his hair, twining them in the strands, pulling so his mouth dipped a little closer to hers. As if she needed his full attention.

She had it. She had always had it. Would always have it.

And then she smiled up at him. Oh Gods, that smile. The naughty thoughts that were so obviously playing in her head reflected in the smile that curled on her lips, making it twist a little to the side as she said, "And the other thing that's wrong is that you are not already balls deep inside me."

He groaned. "Gods, Jules. Where did you learn to talk like that?"

"From the romance books I read."

"Gods bless your romance books."

Then he was kissing her again, hard and fast as he fell

back on the bed pulling her with him. She landed on top of him and the feeling of her splayed against him like that, legs twined, hip to hip, chest to chest, it was glorious. Better than he remembered. But it wasn't enough. "Too many clothes," he said against her lips as his hands moved to push her pyjama top up.

"Too many clothes," she agreed, her lips moving against his before returning to kissing him again. Ye Gods, her kiss. He could never get enough of her kiss. Or her touch. Her fingers were running down his chest, across his stomach, to the top of his board shorts, a bare centimetre away from the tip of his swollen cock.

It flexed, as if it had its own mind and wanted her attention.

And it got it. She cupped it through the material, running her hand up and down its length.

He arched up into her touch, his head dropping back, away from her lips. He sucked in a shuddering breath as she continued the movement. That breath shot out of him a moment later when she shoved her hands down the inside of the fluorescent green and pink board shorts Tam had magicked onto him and her long, fine, strong fingers curled around the stiff length of his cock.

Hells. If she kept that up, he'd explode before he got anywhere close to being balls deep inside her.

He put his hand over hers, stopping her from doing more than squeeze – who knew that would feel so incredibly good? "If you keep doing that, I won't last," he panted roughly.

"That would be a shame." She let go of his cock, but at the same time her head dipped down and she tongued his nipple.

He bucked under the sensation of hot and wet and hard as she licked and then bit him lightly. "Jules!"

She looked up at him, her expression so sexy and knowing, it stole the breath from his lungs. "Yes?" Her brow cocked in a way that made his entire body throb.

"You are going to be the end of me."

"That would be a shame. I don't want to be the end of you. I want to be the start of you." She dipped her head, licked again as she looked up at him in a way that was pure sex and sin. "Hmm, you taste so good." Her hands swept over his stomach, his chest. "Feel so good. I want to taste and feel everything."

"As do I. But we have more than this one time."

She bit her lip, breathing hard. "We do, don't we."

He nodded.

"Then I want you inside me. Now. We'll do the rest next time."

He chuckled as she began to scrabble at the tie on his ridiculous board shorts. "We most certainly will."

Then he began to lift her pyjama top over her head, exposing her breasts to his sight for the first time – handfuls of plump, pink-tipped glory. His mouth dried and he licked his lips. He wanted to taste them. But she was already pulling his shorts down his legs, his cock springing free, and he needed to get her as naked as he was.

He pulled her top so hard, it tore in two. She didn't seem to care – even though they were her favourite summer pyjamas – and then he flipped her over, her breasts bouncing as she landed on the bed. She protested briefly until he hooked his fingers in the waist of her pyjama pants and pulled them off her too, her underpants going with them. He shucked off his shorts a moment later and then they were both naked on the bed together.

She was so beautiful. His skin prickled with awareness of just how incredibly breathtaking she was to him. How perfect the thrust of her breasts, the dip of her waist, the curve of her hips, the feel of her silken, warm skin under his big hands. He didn't know when he'd put his hands on her, but there they were, big and brown against the paleness of her skin. She writhed under his touch, pushing up into his hands as he brushed them up and over her, cupping her breasts as he came down between her legs. He wanted to taste her there at the apex of her thighs – the scent of that warm wetness was so very tantalizing – but the drive to be inside her was pushing him to insanity.

As it was for her too. He could tell. The way she pushed up into him, writhing against his leg, his hip, brushing against his cock. Which wept with the need to be inside her.

He slipped between her legs. She widened them to accommodate him as if it was the most natural thing in the world to her. As if she remembered having done this with him before. Maybe she did. Maybe that's the gift Santa had given them because of his wish. But that was something they could pursue later.

Now, he just needed to be surrounded by her wet, tight, warmth.

Her arms opened to him, welcoming him to her. And as he pushed her legs up and back, giving him more room to move, to go deep, he slid into the tight, wet, warmth of her.

They both moaned with the pleasure of it as he slid slowly, oh so slowly, into that tight embrace. Her hands scrabbled at his shoulders, pulling him closer. She arched her head back, eyes closed.

He didn't like that

"Jules, look at me. I want you to look at me. Need you to look at me."

She tipped her head back, opened her eyes, the blaze of pleasure in them almost his undoing.

"I want more," she said harshly. "I need more." She pushed up into him, taking more of him in.

He pushed in deeper until he could go no further. "Better?"

She nodded.

He began to move. Her eyes fluttered. "Eyes on me."

She did what he asked, their eyes meeting, clinging, their hands grasping together on the bed next to their bodies as he moved deep inside her, sliding in then out. In then out. "Jules. Jules."

"Bas. More. I need more."

He moved faster. Harder. Lifted her legs over his shoulders when it seemed she was ready to take more of him. She writhed, glorious and strong, taking all he had to offer, taking everything he had to give and giving back in turn, her pelvis moving in counterpoint to his movement, gaze never leaving his.

He wanted to kiss her – thought she wanted him to kiss her too as they shared this intimacy – but he wanted to look at her more this first time with this version of Julianna, to watch the expressions of passion and joy on her face, in her eyes.

Then she was lifting up against him, harder, faster, her insides tightening around him, beginning to pulse around him, pushing him on towards his ending, and with a shout of pleasure he was certain could be heard throughout the universe, he let go and they flew into the infinity of loving pleasure together.

More than it had ever been.

Better than it had ever been.

Finally, they were One as the Fates had always meant them to be.

It was the best gift he'd ever been given and when he came down from it, greedy cupid that he was, he wanted more.

Luckily, so did she.

And together, they took it.

FIVE

T am came out of the quick portal he'd created on the other side of the foyer from the stairs that led down into the library. He'd actually been aiming for the library, but it seemed his powers were a little on the fritz today. He shrugged as he began to cross the foyer to the stairs then stopped as some noises he definitely didn't want to hear began to drift down the stairs.

Holy crap! That wasn't what he thought it was, was it? By the sounds of the moaning and loud calling out of names, it definitely was. He clapped his hands over his ears. How was he hearing that through the closed door and all the way down here? It wasn't that he wasn't happy that his parents were getting it on – he was. Well, he was happy *for* them. For him ... he kind of wished he didn't know and definitely couldn't hear what was going on up there.

All children eventually knew that their parents had sex, but knowing that and *knowing* that were two different things entirely. The second was a most definite slap-your-hands-over-your-ears-squeeze-your-eyes-shut-and-scream-lalalalala at the universe sort of thing. He'd been working towards getting them to this point for centuries, so he was happy. But he was also grossed out.

Extremely grossed out.

In fact, maybe it would be better if he actually left Stevens House and left them to it. He had thought to stay down in the library and do a little more research while here, but now he knew his parents were upstairs doing the nasty for the rest of the night and worse, that they were getting louder and louder as they …

Eugh! A little bit of vomit came up into his mouth that he quickly swallowed down.

They were really getting into it. It sounded like they were ramping up and might not just last the night but would keep at it through tomorrow. Not surprising given this was thousands of years in the making but … the thought of that was just—

He shuddered, poking his tongue out and making a 'bleau' noise.

Good for them. Not so good for him.

Especially given, along with the horror of it all, was a fair slice of jealousy. And an aching loneliness he usually didn't allow himself to feel.

Agh! What was he doing? He wasn't the one who was depressed and allowing hopelessness to take him over. He knew love would never come his way so he didn't expect it for himself. As a cupid, he was simply happy to bring it to others. That was his job after all. The thing he'd been born to do. He was perfectly happy with it. Just like all other cupids – aside from Eros and his father of course who were the exceptions – it was not for them to experience a forever love.

He'd thought he'd experienced it once, thousands of years ago, but nothing had come of that. As it shouldn't.

He'd had his duties to take up and she'd had hers. They were never meant to be. He shouldn't have expected more just because his father had broken the curse of being born cupid and managed to find love.

In this instance it wasn't like father like son.

And that was fine.

It was.

Loneliness-shmoneliness. He had too much to do to be lonely. The first of which was getting out of here before he heard more than he already had coming from the bedroom upstairs. The library would protect him from that, so he could still head down there.

Except ...

A stroke of something he really didn't want to feel brushed over his skin.

Gods no! Why hadn't he thought of this? They were two magical people being affected by the magical Spirit of Christmas after all. Their negative emotions had been eking out and affecting things already through the ley-lines. They had expected – and needed – the wish to work so that they would regain positive emotions and send them out to rein-fect the world with better feelings.

Sex was full of positive emotions. Strong positive emotions. The kind of emotions that overrode everything else while a person was lost in their thrall.

Emotions that were now seeping out of his parents and had already made it downstairs to touch him.

"Eugh!" He began to run for the stairs while shuddering violently. It was bad enough to know they were doing the nasty but if he stayed here like he'd planned, he would be hit by the sex-driven emotions emanating from his parents ... So gross.

He crossed the foyer and ran down the stairs into the

library as quickly as he could. If he opened a portal up here, the feelings that were already seeping out might just follow him through. He needed to get down into the safety of the library's stone and wood embrace with the added protection of all that earth above it keeping the sex feelings away from him long enough to make his escape free and clear.

The library ghosts rustled and moaned as he entered the darkened library. It used to be that the lights came on magically whenever anyone entered, but Violetta had dismantled that spell and because this place was secret, she couldn't get an electrician to come in to put the human sensor technology in place so the lights would come on whenever someone entered. While he was beginning to know the library well, Violetta had a habit of moving some of the furniture around, so he couldn't walk around in the dark down here. Thankfully, the light switch was to the right of the archway at the base of the stairs.

He flicked it on and candelabra and wall sconces bloomed to life in the dark, lighting the huge expanse of the library, shining off the ancient grey stone and the beautiful rich mahogany wood of the arched ceiling and the stacks.

The age of this library, the beauty of its design and what it contained stole his breath for a moment as it always did every time he walked into it.

It was truly stupendous, this pantheon of knowledge the Stevens witches had built over the centuries.

One of the ghosts came flying down the nearest stacks, popping out of the end and flaring wide in front of him as if trying to scare him. "Settle down, Hettie. It's only me."

At the sound of his voice she dropped her posturing, a look of delight on her face. She wound around him excitedly, causing his skin to shiver when she accidentally touched him. "Okay, okay. That's enough. I'm happy to see you too. But I can't hang around this time. I have to go and keep searching for the diary." His parents might be together right now, but that didn't mean the curse was actually broken. Clodia wouldn't have made things so simple for them. So while they were doing the wild thing, he'd keep searching.

Hettie zipped back a little way from him, a pout on her translucent pretty face. She'd died young – maybe in her mid-teens – and sometimes struggled to act her actual age and not the age she was when she died. "I promise I'll be back soon," he said. "But I need you to keep an eye on things here for me, okay? Can you do that? You and the other ghosts?"

She nodded eagerly, her image puffed up with what he interpreted to be pride at the fact he was asking her to do something important for him.

"Right, well, I'm going to go now. See you when I get back."

He waved his hand, activating his portal powers. The blue and purple spinning lights circled in front of him, getting bigger as he waved a larger circle with his hand. When it got wide and tall enough, he took a breath and lifted his foot, ready to step through when another portal exploded into life to his left and something flew out of it, almost hitting him.

He ducked and rolled, looking up as he did to see that a reindeer with a huge double rack of antlers with at least twenty points and sporting a red, glowing nose flew over his head. It landed with a skid, managing to stop just before it crashed into the nearest stacks.

On the reindeer's back was an elf wearing the traditional elf-garb of green outfit with candy-striped lederhosen, a jaunty pointed cap sitting on his chestnut brown curls. The elf waved his hand, closing Tam's portal with a snap along with its own, and in a voice that sounded like bells ringing, said, "Where do you think you're going?"

Now on his hands and knees, Tam blinked at him, unable to find any words at the sudden appearance of Rudolph and one of Santa's elves. And not any old elf. This elf was Santa's right hand elf.

Gary Elfman.

"Don't just stand there looking stupid, Tamuel," Gary said, slinging his leg over Rudolph's back and sliding down and onto the floor. "I've come a long way and could do with a cuppa."

Tam blinked at the elf as he marched past and into the library's kitchen. He really wanted to get out of here before the sex emotions made it down to the library – they would do so soon given how fast those emotion-driven sexy feelings had moved from Jules' room and through the big house, down the stairs and into the foyer. Which meant he really needed to get whatever this was wrapped up as soon as possible. Especially given he really didn't want Gary or Rudolph here when the energy made it down to the library. He'd paired up a few elves in his time and had seen what happened when they let go – it really wasn't pretty. He'd been scarred for years by what he'd seen them do.

And don't get him started on Santa's reindeer. Those boys and girls could party in a way that was everything naughty and nothing particularly nice.

He shuddered. "Umm, maybe you could just tell me what brings you here. I actually have places to go, things to do."

Gary waved at him impatiently. "All in good time, cupid. You know we elves like to talk over tea. Besides, Rudolph is a bit thirsty."

A nudge in his back had him looking over his shoulder at the reindeer who stood behind him. Rudolph waggled his head, seeming to urge Tam to follow Gary into the kitchen. In fact, he seemed a little insistent about it. He nudged him again, harder this time, almost making Tam fall flat on his face.

Tam hurriedly pushed to his feet to do as the reindeer bid before he could 'nudge' him again. Despite the happy spin that legend and song had given Rudolph, the reindeer could be vicious in the protection of Santa and his elves and in the name of protecting the Spirit of Christmas in all its forms. One didn't ignore one of Santa's reindeer if he appeared in front of you and demanded you do something.

Maybe if he told them about what was going on upstairs he could ... but no. That was a conversation he simply didn't want to have with an elf and a reindeer. It actually wasn't a conversation he wanted to have full stop. If he just got them refreshments then they'd get to the point of them being here and he would still be able to get out of here before things got bad.

Fully aware of the reindeer following along behind, its hooves clip-clopping along the floor jauntily, he hurried into the kitchen, overtaking Gary before he made it to the sink, grabbed the kettle from the bench, filled it and put it on. Then turning around he asked, "Chai or Orange Pekoe?"

"Do you have any wet chai? And oat milk? I've become a bit lactose intolerant."

Tam blinked at him for a moment and then said, "Umm, yeah, I think we do." He went to the fridge, pulled out the oat milk Violetta kept there for guests then went to the tea pantry and pulled down the container of wet chai Jules made herself. It took him a moment to find the chai steeper and to realise he no longer needed the kettle on. He turned it off, poured oat milk into the silver barista's jug and used the steamer wand on the coffee machine to heat the oat milk and froth it a little.

"Take a seat," he said over his shoulder at the elf as he stood in the middle of the kitchen behind him.

"Some of those lemon biscuits would be nice too," Gary said. "I missed out on morning tea coming here. And do you have some carrots for Rudolph? He's rather partial to the baby ones if you have them. With the green attached if possible."

"Sure," Tam said, still baffled as to what both of them were doing here. Particularly now. But he also knew he wouldn't be able to question Gary until he'd got him the biscuits and chai and put down a bucket of water and a plate of carrots for Rudolph.

He was a little thankful that Gary and Rudolph hadn't come out of their portal in the foyer and made him go to the kitchen upstairs. There would have been no escaping the sex feelings up there. Right now he had a little time. Not much, but some. He shuddered again.

"You okay?" Gary asked from behind him.

"Just a little cold," he said as he finished frothing the oat milk and put the chai in to steep.

"You should put something warmer on. Although, I'm finding it a little hot in here," the elf said.

"Probably because you come from one of the coldest places on Earth."

"Maybe. Although the workshop and house are always kept snuggly warm. Santa has a bit of an issue with the cold – he gets chilblains."

Rudolph made some snorting noise and Gary chuckled. "You're right there, Rudi. I wish he'd wash his red long-johns more often too. Although his red-leopard G-strings

Mrs Claus likes him to wear on sexy days are worse. Those things get truly funky smelling when he turns the heat up too much."

Tam swallowed back a gag. "That's information I really don't need to know."

"You're telling me," Gary said wryly. "Try being the one who has to wash his precious smalls."

Tam gagged again. "Living the high-life."

"I surely am," Gary said wryly. "Which is why I'm here."

"To gross me out by telling me about Santa's stinky underwear?"

SIX

Gary and Rudolph both made chortling sounds. "Hardly. That's just a bonus," Gary said when he stopped chortling.

Tam sighed and rubbed his brow, then picked up the jug of chai, grabbed a strainer and poured Gary a mug. "Honey?" he asked over his shoulder.

"Yes please."

Rudolph made a hooting sound.

"Rudi would like honey too."

Tam turned to face them. "I'm making Rudolph an oat milk chai too?"

"Yep," Gary said with a smug smile on his face. "Although he'll have it in a bowl and you can add four fingers of spiced rum to his as well if you've got some handy. I promised him a treat if he brought me here and he is rather partial to oat milk chai with spiced rum. His brothers and sisters prefer whiskey, but he has always liked to be different."

"Right." Of course he did. Although, it kind of made sense that Rudolph and the other reindeer liked spirits.

Santa was a tea-totaller from October through to Christmas day, so it had always seemed strange to him that it had become such a thing to leave some kind of spirit out for him to drink. It was probably the reindeer who dropped that little titbit into the social-mind zeitgeist so the locals would leave glasses of whiskey out for 'Santa' when it was in fact for them.

Of course, fathers the world over used it as an excuse to sit and eat cookies and have a dram of whatever floated their boats, so if it was the reindeer who had spread that rumour, it had backfired on them. Sucks to be them.

Five minutes later, he placed a plate of carrots in front of Rudolph – he'd pulled them through a portal from the kitchen upstairs – as well as his bowl of chai with a good swig of spiced rum in it – he'd portalled the rum from the lounge room spirit trolley – then placed a plate of lemon biscuits in front of Gary who was already sipping on his chai with a happy smile on his face.

"Mmm, I like this chai. What is it?"

"It's a blend Jules makes. She's got a knack for blending teas."

"It's lovely. Can you give me some to take back to the North Pole with me? I bet Mrs Claus would love this."

"Sure," Tam said, taking a seat opposite Gary, trying to ignore the slurping coming from Rudolph over the other side of the table. "So, you were saying you came here for ...?"

Gary swallowed another mouthful. "Ah, yes. My reason for being here is threefold."

He took another sip of his drink and sighed then picked up a lemon biscuit and took a bite. "Delightful," he said around a mouthful.

Tam's leg was jiggling up and down under the table and he put his hand on it, pushing it down before he began to give his impatience away. Elves didn't respond well to impatience. They had their own way of doing things and things were always done in their own time, not yours. Pushing them on it would only put you on their naughty list. And you didn't want to end up on their naughty list. Especially as an adult.

So he took a swig of the generous shot of spiced rum he'd poured himself – he needed something to get through this – and waited while Gary finished his biscuit and took another.

Rudolph lifted his head and made some querying sound. "You won't want one of these," Gary said to him, waving a biscuit around in the air. "Citrus always gives you the runs."

Rudolph snorted and pawed the floor.

"Fine. But you know you can't go here, so you'll have to hold it in until we get home." Gary looked over at Tam and said out the side of his mouth, "Santa's reindeer poo is steeped with magical flying dust – it enables them to fly – so they're forbidden to poop anywhere but in the special latrine at home where the flying dust is separated from the actual poop. So you don't have to worry about him dumping a load on your library carpet."

"What a relief," Tam said, head reeling with more information he really didn't want to know. He took a large swig of his drink, swallowing all of it down, and forced his leg to stop knocking against the bottom of the table again.

He wasn't sure whether it was the warmth of the spirits or because the sex energy had actually begun to make it down here already, but he was starting to feel a bit better. Looser.

He eyed Rudolph and Gary to see if they felt it too. Rudolph seemed happier as he finished off his bowl of chai and turned to the carrots, but Gary didn't seem any different from when he arrived on the reindeer's back.

So maybe it was just the spirits. Thank small mercies for that.

"So," Gary said, finally finishing his chai and the plate of biscuits. "As I was saying, the reason I am here is threefold."

Tam raised his brows and sat forward a little.

"One," Gary said, raising a finger. "I needed a break from my sister who has been nagging me to do the dishes at home." He made a grimace. "I love her, I really do, but she just doesn't know when to let a thing go. I mean, it's my busiest time of year getting Santa ready for the big night and all. I don't have time to do the dishes even if she is the one that has been doing all the cooking and our deal is whoever cooks doesn't have to do the dishes. I mean, she doesn't have half my work at this time of year, so it's not too much to ask that she just takes care of the dishes too for December. That's fair, right?"

"Uhm ..." Tam said, trying to figure out how this was important to him. "Yeah, sure."

"I thought so too." Gary sighed then raised a second finger. "Three."

"Don't you mean two?"

"What?"

Tam gestured at the two fingers. "You have only told me one reason why you're here. Now you're up to two."

Gary pursed his lips. "Well, truth be told, two isn't really important. Rudolph's just been bitching to get away for the last weeks – Blitzen is being an annoying arse as usual and nobody can make him stop. So, let's jump to three, shall we?"

Tam shrugged as nonchalantly as he could. Gary getting to the point was all he wanted because he was becoming pretty certain that the goofy look starting to cross Rudolph's face was because the sexual energy had indeed made its way down here. "Sure."

Gary's wide mouth split into an ear-to-ear grin. "Great. Three." He held a third finger up. "Santa wants to see you."

Tam blinked at him for a moment. "He what?"

"He wants to see you."

Tam shook his head. He could hear the words but they still didn't make sense. "Santa wants to see me? Now?"

"Yes now," Gary said impatiently. "Otherwise I wouldn't be here. I thought I made that clear."

"Right. Yep. Sure. Santa wants to see me now."

Rudolph made a hooting noise again and Gary nodded slowly. "Yeah, I think you're right. It's affecting him much faster than I thought it would. It's strong stuff. We really should get out of here sooner rather than later before it affects us more than it already has. I really don't have the time or energy to participate in an elf orgy right now."

Rudolph made a sound of agreement. Gary chuckled. "I'm with you there."

"What?" Tam asked, looking between them – had they just been talking about sex? Did they know what was going on upstairs? For that matter, had Gary's cheeks begun to go a little red rather than their usually rosy, pink-tinted freckle-dusted hue?

"Nothing you want to know about. Unless you're interested in the sexual practices of over-stimulated reindeer."

"Nope," Tam said, shaking his head rapidly. "Nope, not interested at all."

"Didn't think so," Gary said smugly then he stood up. "So, let's get going, shall we?"

"Now?" Tam asked again.

Gary rolled his little black eyes. "Yes, now," he said very

slowly as if talking to a child who was only just learning to talk.

"But ... isn't this the time of year that Santa doesn't like unexpected visitors?"

"You won't be unexpected. He did ask for you after all."

"Oh, umm, of course. Of course," Tam said as he tried to wrap his mind around the request. Nobody visited Santa at this time of year. Nobody outside his elves, reindeer and Mrs Claus. But here was Gary telling him that Santa had requested to see him. "So ... when we go there ... to the North Pole ... I'll get the pass."

"The pass?"

Tam nodded. "The one that means I won't be savaged by Rudolph's angry brethren for disturbing Santa at his busiest time of the year."

Gary and Rudolph began to chortle again. "Pass. There's no pass," Gary managed to say around his laughter. "That's just a story the reindeer began centuries ago to try and keep unwanted visitors from traipsing into Santa's Village bothering us all. I can't believe you thought it was real."

"What? But Eros makes such a fuss of having to get the pass every time he has had to send a cupid to Santa's Village." Gary and Rudolph laughed harder. "I don't see what's so funny about this," Tam said, trying to reign in his temper which was suddenly too quick to rise — just like every emotion seemed ready to rise at the smallest provocation. Shit, he really was being affected by his parents' sexual energy. He stood up abruptly. "Fine. There's no pass. So let's just go, shall we."

Gary tipped his head. "Sure." He ran over to Rudolph who was now standing to attention, his red nose glowing, eyes swirling faster and faster with all the colours of a nebula. The elf leapt up onto Rudolph's back then held out his hand for Tam. "What are you doing standing over there. Get on."

"Umm, can't I just walk through the portal next to you?"

"You could … if you wanted to be torn apart by the security net that's up around the village."

"Security net?"

"Of course. The pass story doesn't work to keep some eager beavers away, so we came up with a better way to turn them back."

"A security net?"

"Uh-huh. It's kind of like a shield, but it bounces them back to where they originally came from with no memory of the journey."

"Then why would it tear me apart?"

"Because you'll be coming in fast and hot through this particular portal. If you were walking in like most intruders through your own portals, you'd just be bounced back. But coming in the way we'll be going in a reindeer portal which is the only way to get through the net …" Gary grimaced and sucked in a breath between his teeth. "It's nasty unless you're riding with the reindeer who created it. And when I say riding with, I mean either in the sleigh behind them or on the back of one of them. So climb on."

"He won't mind me riding on his back," Tam said, pointing at Rudolph who had bared his teeth at Tam when he took a step towards them.

"Oh, don't mind him. His bark's worse than his bite."

"Excuse me if I don't want to take your word for it," Tam said, holding back even though his skin was now prickling with an awareness he really didn't want to contemplate – especially given Gary was starting to look mighty good looking.

Gary sighed. "Rudolph. Stop being sexually aggressive. You know the feeling isn't truly coming from you. And Tam isn't going to vie with you for one of the female reindeer at home. So stop messing with him and let him on your back. You know how bad things are about to get if we take much longer."

Rudolph made a grunty-moaney sound and nodded Tam forward. His teeth were still bared though, so Tam made his way over and clambered on behind Gary very carefully.

"Hold on tight," Gary said. "The ride in can be wild."

A portal spun into existence in front of them and Tam gripped onto Gary just as Rudolph leapt forward into the portal and flew through the maelstrom within it that led to the North Pole.

CHAPTER
SEVEN

B as opened his eyes slowly blinking against the bright light shining through the bedroom window. The light seemed strange. As did the fact he was lying under the sheets in the bed and wasn't curled up at the foot of it like he did on the rare occasions that Jules had a sleep in and he was able to join her after his change magic had fully dissipated.

Given the slant of the sun across the bed, this was one of those mornings. In the past, it had been an unusual occurrence for Jules – she was a morning person and was usually up by six-thirty, earlier in summer. Recently though, as her depression had deepened, she had been getting up later and later and sleeping at her feet had become a regular occurrence. If he hadn't been so exhausted himself from the increasingly difficult change from man into cat, he would have been more concerned faster than he had been.

Although, this time, her need to sleep in wasn't caused by deepening depression. Given the exertion of last night he wasn't surprised she needed more rest. It was kind of amazing he was awake.

They'd made love. Multiple times. Throughout the night.

He smiled lazily, self-indulgently, warmth filling him at the—

They'd made love. Multiple times!

He jerked upright. Or, he would have if not for the fact that his arms were full of the warm softness that could only be a woman.

His woman.

His love.

His Jules.

She muttered a protest at his jerking movement. He stilled and she quickly settled down, nuzzling her cheek into his chest. Her hair tickled his chin and she was snoring very softly as she did whenever she had exhausted herself. One hand was curled over his heart next to her chin and the other lay down beside her hip, incredibly close to his groin.

His very man-like groin.

He wasn't in his cat form as he should be after dawn. He was still a man. And he could see!

By the Gods ... it had worked! The wish to Santa had worked better than he'd ever imagined it could. He had wanted to believe it would work to rid Jules of her depression, but there had been a part of him that hadn't allowed himself to think it could possibly be true. Luck had not been on his side for many, many years. But now luck seemed to be his best friend. Because not only had Jules lifted out of her depression and hopelessness – as his had the moment hers did – but she remembered she loved him. She'd kissed him and enticed him as only Jules could do and then they'd made love.

Mad, wild, glorious love for the rest of the night.

If that had been all he'd got out of the wish to Santa, he would have been a happy man. He would have lived on memories of it over the next few months, clinging to the joy of it, letting memory alone drive him on to ensure they did all they could to break the curse that the evil High Priestess witch Clodia had placed on them thousands of years ago.

Memory of last night would have been enough to keep the hopelessness that had been plaguing him from taking him over once more. It would have been more than enough to get him through to Valentine's Eve. It would have fired his belief that they could break the curse and be together forever as the Fates had always meant them to be. It alone would have made him certain they would find the diary and that Jules would discover all she needed to follow the path that would allow them to break the curse – because it could not be broken without her knowing something of her past life and the curse she was under.

But now it seemed the wish had given him even more than he'd hoped for. It had stopped him from turning into a cat during the day. It had given him his sight back while he was a man. It had kept Jules in his arms right through dawn and into the morning.

What else might it have given him?

He shoved that question aside – he couldn't allow himself to hope for more than this. Didn't want to push the wish past what it naturally contained. Didn't want to risk undoing whatever this was and losing even a second of what time he had left with her like this.

How long did he have?

No. He couldn't even let himself seek an answer for that. Because the Goddess of Luck – Fortuna in the Roman pantheon Jules' family was tied to, or Tyche in the Greek

Pantheon of his father – might seem to be on his side right now, but she could turn from him at any moment. She had done so before in spectacular fashion. He didn't want to ask too many questions and force her favourable gaze from him too quickly.

He wanted to hold onto this for as long as he could have it.

His arms tightened convulsively around Jules as she lay, gloriously naked, draped along his side and across his chest, her warm, soft breasts pressing erotically into him, the curling hair at the apex of her thighs brushing his hip.

His cock twitched, but not just because he wanted her again – and he did. Every time, in each incarnation, the moment she reached adulthood, his attachment to her as a guardian with its familial love had changed into the love of passion and need exactly as it had been from the moment he'd laid eyes on Julianna Stevius two thousand years ago. But because of the curse, she had never seen him as more than the man who was bound to their family for some unknown reason, who lived in their house as a cat during the day and a blind man at night. It wasn't until this reincarnation that she had started to embrace him as a friend – something she had never done before.

For himself though, the moment she became an adult, he wanted her passionately, wanted to hear her cry out his name with that husky throb in her voice again and again as she'd done when she'd been Julianna Stevius. He had always held it back though, his love and need for her unrequited until the curse was broken. But it had always been there, horribly, necessarily repressed, hurting him with the effort to hold it back.

Hurting him through the curse every time he let any ounce of it show.

But now ... last night ... It had exploded out of him, no longer unrequited but fully, satisfyingly expressed and appreciated by the one person in the world he wanted to appreciate it.

Thousands of years of pushing it down, of hiding it, of wishing and longing and imagining and yet nothing he had imagined over all those years could have prepared him for the actuality of once more being with this woman who was his mate.

It had been explosive. It had been so sizzling hot it was a wonder the bed hadn't turned to cinders. And yet tenderness had been there alongside the passion, deep and utter love and caring for the pleasure of the other, making every moment, every sensation, even more special.

He wanted to fall into the magnificence of it again. But he also didn't want to lose this moment of waking with her in his arms. The thought of rolling her over and sliding into her wet warmth again was ever present in his mind, but while that want was there, so was this want, this *need*, to be here with her like this. Just holding her as she slept.

It was the most amazing thing. She'd never really slept in his arms when she was Julianna all those centuries ago and he was a naive, love-stricken cupid. Their love-trysts had by necessity been brief. She'd always had to return to Vesta's temple to sleep in the dorm alongside her priestess sisters. They'd only ever been able to snatch moments to be together, never spending an entire night.

He'd imagined what it might be like though. Often. Over the centuries while he'd been trapped by the curse to live with each incarnation of her and her family, spending his days as her cat familiar and his nights as a blind man, longing to see her and hold her and be with her, but unable to do so because the curse wouldn't allow it, those imaginings were what had kept him sane. They had been his—

His eyes snapped open as he sucked in a breath.

The curse!

If he was here with Jules in this way, did it mean that the curse was broken? Had the Christmas wish to Santa Claus been so strong that it had broken the curse? Could Santa do that?

He had no idea. Up until last night, he hadn't even thought Santa was real. He'd been a myth.

He felt kind of stupid now not to realise the jolly white bearded, red coated man was real. Cupids were real even though most people thought them myths. Gods, Goddesses, witches, magic ... all real even though for most people they were the province of myth and legend. Of course Santa was real. He was Saint Nicholas. A real fourth century Greek bishop from Myra in what was now called Türkiye who somehow, because of his good deeds, charity and kindness, had apparently become something like a God. At least in so far as belief powered him and enabled him to keep kindness and hope alive in the world.

That belief had been deepened within the popular zeitgeist when Dutch legends of Sinterklaas melded with English traditions of Father Christmas among others. The melding had culminated in a poem by an unknown author in the late 1800s and the legend of the modern day Santa Claus and his flying reindeer was fully cemented into popular culture. This was helped along by a soft drink brand in the 1900s which used its synonymous red and white branding in his coat and beard, gave him a jolly big belly and red cheeks, and with clever marketing turned him into something more than the whole Christian world believed in. After that, belief in him soared. It had never dawned on him before to think what that might do even if he truly had been a myth. That kind of belief was enough to bring myth into reality with a little magical help. Given he had already been a real man, of course that kind of belief would make him even more powerful than he was before.

But powerful enough to break their curse?

He had no idea. Maybe Tam would know. He'd have to find the young cupid today some time and ask him. Hopefully he hadn't run too far away when trying to escape the effects of the sexual energy they put out last night. Holy Hells. He hadn't though about it until now, but nobody in this house could have missed the energy that had pulsed from them, filled with everything they were experiencing together. It had been so strong it had probably caused a number of rather raunchy nights to happen in their neighbours' houses.

He couldn't be sorry for that though. Some of the couples who lived around them needed a good night of raunch.

He certainly had.

His smile widened, his happiness bursting to life inside him. He had Jules in his arms. Finally. After thousands of years of torturous waiting.

He would do everything he could to keep her there. If it meant sending wishes to Santa Claus every day until he was certain the curse had indeed been broken, then he would do it. He'd prostrate himself at the feet of Saint Nick if it came to that. He'd do more than that. He'd do anything. He'd do everything.

Because this ... this ... He didn't want to lose it. Not ever again.

He ran his hand over Jules' naked back. By all that was holy, her skin was soft! And warm. And pliable in just the right kind of way. And the scent rising from her warm, soft skin ... it was a mix of all the scents of Christmas that she loved – cinnamon, cardamom, nutmeg and pine, citrus and ginger and that perfect sweetness that arose whenever she cooked her gingernut cookies at this time of year. Or put her Christmas fruit cake on to bake. He hadn't realised how much those scents had become hers over the years.

His brow furrowed. Actually, he couldn't remember her smelling as intensely like Christmas yesterday. Her scent had muted, changed over the last few months but now ... Now it was even richer than it had been before.

She smelled amazing. She had always smelled amazing, but now he wanted to lick up that scent. In fact, he wanted to eat her up and—

She moaned huskily and moved sinuously against him, her breasts rubbing erotically against the skin covering his ribs. Oh, holy Gods! Her nipples were hard and erect. And suddenly he became aware of another scent joining the Christmassy one that was exuding from her. This scent was spicier, hotter and a little musky – the scent of her sex. He could almost taste the wetness of her behind those curls that were now rubbing against his hip. Up and down and up and down. In time to the hand that was rubbing over his very puckered nipple.

He looked down at her.

She was awake. And smiling up at him with a very naughty smile on her lips, her eyes still a little sleepy but full of heated desire that was likely to set him on fire if he stared into the depths of them for too long.

"Good morning," she said, her voice a husky whisper.

"Good morning," he said, his voice equally husky.

The hand down by his side moved to cup his very erect cock. He hissed in a breath as she curled her fingers around the length of him and squeezed. "Will it be a good morning?" she asked, brow arched provocatively.

"Oh, I hope it will be a very good morning," he said as he flipped her over onto her back, delighting in her excited squeal.

She looked up at him – it was an astonishing feeling to look right back at her as he hovered over her. "Kiss me," she demanded.

"That's exactly what I plan." He backed up this promise by moving down her body, kissing every single warm, silken inch of her. She squirmed and arched under him until he got to the wet deliciousness of her pussy. He looked up at her before he did what he'd longed to do since waking. Her breasts were moving up and down fast, her breaths coming in harsh pants. "I'm going to lick you up until you scream."

"Stop talking ... about it," she panted. "And just ... do it."

"With pleasure," he said and licked long and hard up the wet core of her. She writhed and moaned. He licked again, holding her hips to keep her exactly where he wanted her as he licked and sucked and nibbled the sweetness of her core. He kept going, moving one hand from her hip so he could push his finger deep inside her, one, then another, then another, pumping in and out to the time of his licks. He kept going until she screamed his name and pulsed so hard around the fingers he had inside of her that he thought she might never come down.

Wanting to feel her orgasm around his painfully hard cock, he crawled back up her body, and as he bent to taste her pink nipples, he slid inside her, shouting her name against her flesh as her orgasm intensified again, pulsing around him long and hard. So hard it was almost painful to move inside her, her internal muscles gripping him so tightly.

But he did move.

He moved for her pleasure. Moved for his. And too soon – far too soon – his balls tightened so hard they almost drew up inside him and he lost himself to his release deep inside her, calling out her name as she called out his.

And as their shouts became echoes around them, as the orgasmic pulses faded away, he held her tight to him and knew he never wanted to let her go.

He would truly do anything not to lose this again.

EIGHT

Jules didn't know anyone could feel as good as she did when she woke up for the second time still wrapped in Bas' arms.

They'd made love. For what remained of last night after Bas came to her and again this morning. Multiple times.

Her smile widened. She felt rather like the cat that had got all the cream and then some.

Speaking of cats, why wasn't Bas in his cat form?

She had a feeling she should be more concerned about that, but honestly right now, she couldn't muster anything but a distant curiosity.

And gratitude. Lots of gratitude for the fact that he was still in his man form – and what a man!

She wasn't sure how her smile widened even more, but it did. She was so glad that he hadn't turned into the cat again. She loved the cat version of him too, but the man version ... well, he had brought her pleasure in ways she didn't know were possible. She hoped that he wouldn't stop. Hoped even more fervently that she could return the pleasure. She was well aware that he'd had a pretty amazing time making love to her too, but she wanted to explore ways she could bring him pleasure like he'd done for her. It only seemed fair.

If he wasn't so soundly asleep right now, she'd do some pleasuring of her own – she had thoughts about it. Lots of thoughts. The kind of thoughts she'd never had before about anyone, let alone Bas. Until last night. Last night something had unravelled inside her – and in him – and she had felt things she didn't think she would ever feel. For anyone. Let alone her best friend.

It was kind of incredible.

Even more incredible was the certainty that he shared her feelings. She wanted to wake him up, to ask him if he'd always felt that way about her or if it was a newly awakened thing like it was for her. But he was sleeping and he needed his sleep. He'd certainly not got any sleep last night. Not that she'd had much, but she'd at least had a few hours before he'd woken her up in such a delicious way this morning.

So it was best to let him sleep a little longer. He often slept the morning away after turning into the cat. The change was quite tiring for him – and had become even more so over the last few months.

Of course, he hadn't changed, so that wasn't what was making him sleep the morning away. No – her smile widened – she was fully to blame for that.

Speaking of morning, was it even morning anymore? She had no idea. It was still daylight, but what time?

Did it matter?

She was happy to stay here with him like this all day and night, forever and ever. Making love. With her best friend. Her lover.

Her lover.

Bas was her lover.

She loved him. And he loved her.

He loved her!

And he always would according to the words he'd said over and over again last night and again this morning.

As she had always loved him.

She'd thought the love had only been a friend love. But it wasn't. She was wrong to think that these feelings were new for her before. When that thing had broken open inside of her last night the feelings she'd kept hidden deep inside herself, from him, from herself even – feelings that had always been there – had come roaring out. And she'd been unable to stop herself from acting on them. And he'd reciprocated big time.

It hadn't mattered that she'd always thought she didn't deserve love, especially with someone like him. It didn't matter that she'd come to believe that she had obviously done something at some time to make the Fates remove the weave in her lifethreads that gave people their one true love.

All that had mattered in that moment was that she felt these feelings, that passion and desire for him. It had been overwhelming.

And had become even more so when he'd responded like she'd never imagined anyone responding to her. Because he loved her too.

Like she loved him.

It was incredible. As incredible as making love to him. Mind blowing. In the best way ever.

If this was what it was like for other people, how on earth did they ever manage to make it out of bed? She quite simply didn't want to move. Unless of course it was to climb on top of him and try out some of the naughty, sexy things she had flashing through her mind right now.

She realised she was moving her hand over his chest, finger circling his nipple, and froze. She hadn't meant to do that because she didn't want to disturb his slumber.

It seemed she had very little control over her body when it came to Bas.

Her Bas.

Always her Bas.

Forever her Bas.

She could never be without him again. If she was forced to part from him, she thought she might die.

Breath hitched in her throat and she realised she was frowning. Tears were running down her face. What the Hells? Why was she crying?

She brushed the tears aside with the back of her hand before they could land on his naked chest. She didn't want him to know she was upset. Because she didn't know why she was upset.

She shouldn't be upset. Not after the night she'd just shared with the most amazing man she'd ever met.

And yet ... the tears wouldn't stop. And the feeling inside her ... Ugh. What was that? It certainly had nothing in common with the happy glow she'd woken with only moments ago. This was ... this was ... like the most horrible pain tearing at her heart. Like unbearable loss. Like horrific, all-encompassing grief that threatened to drag her down into the depths of Tartarus.

A sob escaped her lips – a raw, ragged sound that echoed through the quiet bedroom. Ah Goddess, what was going on?

She rolled away from Bas, extricating herself from his arms, but that seemed to make it worse because another sob escaped her lips, this one louder and more violent, making her chest and shoulders shake. It was quickly followed by another one, and another. She clapped her hand to her mouth, trying to stop them from coming, but there was no stopping them.

Bas shifted behind her, making waking sounds.

She pushed off the bed, meaning to get away from him. He couldn't see her like this. She didn't want him to know she was upset. He'd want to know why and she couldn't tell him. Couldn't even explain it to herself. And she definitely didn't want him to think it had anything to do with him or what they'd shared last night. Because it didn't. That had only brought her joy. So much joy.

So why wasn't she feeling the joy anymore?

She wanted the joy back. Why couldn't she have it back?

The yawning sense of loss and grief stretched wider inside her. She trembled under the weight of it, stumbling as she tried to make it to the door. She had to get out of this room before she woke Bas with this nonsense.

Because it was nonsense. It had to be nonsense. There was no reason to feel like this. She'd had tragedy in her life – she'd lost her parents in one horrible car accident – but even that hadn't felt like this. That grief had gentled over the years. It was always there, but it didn't feel like she might lose herself to it.

It had never felt like she'd lose herself to it.

Not like this.

This grief ... this loss ... she was glad she didn't have to put up with it for much longer. Glad she didn't have to live with the loss of her love and her son for much longer.

Glad she was going to die soon.

She slammed through the door and stumbled into the

wall opposite as that thought hit her. She wasn't going to die soon! What was she thinking? It was like ... it was like ... it had been someone else's thought. Someone else's memory. Someone else's ...

"Jules. Jules. It's okay. Let it go. Just let it go."

Bas' warm, strong arms wrapped around her, lifting her from the floor where she'd crumbled – when had she crumbled to the floor? – holding her close. His scent, spicy and citrus with a bit of something deeper, like fresh cut wood, wrapped around her as firmly as his arms did, slipping inside her with every sob.

Ah Goddess! She was still sobbing. Couldn't seem to stop. Her entire body was wracked by them and she could barely breathe. Her chest ached. Her head pounded. Her heart thundered in her chest.

She wanted it to stop. Wanted it to stop. Wanted it all just to stop.

"Jules. Jules. Please. Come back to me. Let go of the memory. I'm here. I'm here now. You won't lose me. You'll never lose me again. Come back to me. Now."

Sebastio – her Bas as she called him ... his arms tightened around her, held her strongly but gently. So gentle. Always so gentle with her even when the sex was wild and frenzied because they couldn't get enough of each other in the brief moments they had together.

She had thought he was her everything, that they would be together forever because the Goddess was bound to bless such a strong, loving union filled only with goodness, no matter of the vows to the Goddess Vesta that had been made on her behalf before she was old enough to speak them. There was nothing bad here, only good. The kind of good that would seep out into the world, into the universe, and affect others with the love, passion, empathy and friendship they felt for each other.

Because he was her best friend. Always, now and forever.

And he was her greatest love. Always, now and forever.

What was better than that? What could create better vibes to flow out into the universe than that? Who could possibly say that this was wrong? Who could possibly see evil in this?

Except ... except ... someone had. Clodia had. Her High Priestess. The woman she'd always looked up to as almost a mother. A slightly scary, demanding mother, but still a mother after she was torn from her own mother's arms when she was but a baby.

Clodia had found them together and bespelled them both before Bas could get away as she had screamed at him to do. The High Priestess had taken them into custody, accused them of horrible things, made it seem like they were bad, like they were evil, like they would bring destruction to *Roma* because they'd had the hubris to fall in love.

And in falling in love, in making love, she'd broken her vows as far as Clodia was concerned and become traitor to not only Vesta, but to all of *Roma*.

The senate had pronounced sentence on both of them even though they had no authority over Bas, and they had been given over to Clodia for the ultimate punishment for such treason: death.

But Clodia had something else in mind. She had tried to steal Julianna's magic after she'd given birth to her son, using the birth energy as part of her spell. She had cursed both of them and their love as she did so. And then she had thrown her into the opening to the burial cell and dumped all the earth into the opening in one, violent go, forcing Julianna to crawl into the cell she was to die in.

It was a traditional death, reserved for Vestal Virgins who broke their virginal vows. Vestal Virgins could not be hung or beheaded like other criminals of the state, because they were sacred. It would bring the evil eye to *Roma* if anyone hurt or killed or put hands on a Vestal Virgin. So they dug out an entrance and a cell under the earth, placed just enough furniture in there for it to be considered an apartment and left food and water – three to four days usually – and then buried the entrance to the 'apartment' with the Vestal Virgin inside. Because she was alive and unhurt when she went in there, the belief was that they didn't 'kill' her.

But of course, they never checked if she was alive or dead. The newer part of her mind had a term for that. Schrodinger's Cat. One did not know if the cat in the box was alive or dead until the box lid was lifted. If you never lifted the lid of the box, then the cat could be both dead and alive, living in both states at once. It was a theory they had let them get away with murder because nobody with any reason could think that the Vestal Virgin who was buried alive in the 'apartment' underground could last longer than the three to four days – they would run out of air long before they ran out of food.

She had. She'd suffocated slowly and painfully. She could still remember it now. The air had filled with thick dust from the dirt that was dumped in the entrance, making it hard to breathe right from the very beginning. It got into her lungs, those fine filaments, her entire body racked with coughs, between which she gasped for breath.

She had longed to just fall asleep. Had been told that's what happened to those who had undergone this punishment before her. As they drew in less and less oxygen, they just drifted into sleep and died painlessly.

That hadn't been the way it happened for her. She thought maybe that had been part of Clodia's curse, to ensure she would remain awake the entire time and remember all she had lost as she died slowly, painfully. Her grief over the loss of her baby that had been torn from her arms just after its birth had been something terrible to endure. As was the pain of knowing her cupid lover had been cursed by the evil High Priestess witch, always aware that he could never be with the love of his life in any of her incarnations. And there was the ragged gaping hole inside her where her powers had once been. Goddess gifted at birth, they'd been torn from her by the worst kind of evil spell by the very High Priestess she thought she could trust with her life. She hadn't known – how could she – that Clodia had such evil intentions; that she'd only ever been kind to her because she had machinations to steal Julianna's power?

That ancient incarnation of her, Julianna Stevius, Lianna as she was known to her friends, had sat there in her grief and pain, her breathing becoming shallow and her heart pounding loud in her ears, slowing, slowing, so painful, filling her up with nothing but emptiness.

She'd begged for unconsciousness, to be given the blessing of falling asleep before death took her. But it hadn't happened. She'd been aware the moment she'd gasped her last breath and her heart had taken its last, sluggish, painful thump. She'd stared at the bare walls as her life came to a stop, and knew she would be alone for eternity.

For she had been cursed to never love or be loved by the one man she'd thought could be her everything.

That feeling of helplessness, of hopelessness had followed her into death and painted her soul throughout the thousands of years and multiple reincarnations since. She suddenly remembered every single one of them. Always powerless. Surrounded by family. Her love always there but she could never truly see him; never truly recognize him. Until …

Until now.

Now she saw him. Now she was with him in the way the Fates had meant for her to be with him.

She had made love to him! Multiple times.

The wonder of it filled her and, as it did, the hopelessness and despair flew away. She looked up at him through tear-blurred eyes and all she knew was love. For him. And all she could see in his eyes was his love for her.

He was her one and always.

Except …

How was that possible with the curse intact?

CHAPTER

NINE

She should not be able to feel love for him, just like all the other incarnations had never felt love for him. And yet, she did.

What had changed?

What had made it so she did remember what they had shared? What she felt for him.

Did Bas know what had happened?

She blinked rapidly, trying to rid herself of the tears, wanting to see him clearly now she remembered. Now she knew.

He was looking at her – actually looking at her. She hadn't really taken it in last night, hadn't really fully appreciated what it had meant – because she hadn't remembered any of it then. But he'd never been able to look at her when he was in his human form, because part of the curse had been that he could never look upon her with his human eyes. But now, he was looking at her with his beautiful peridot eyes, so much like the colour they'd been when he was in his cat form, except with splashes of vivid blue through the yellow-green.

Alongside the love she'd noted only moments ago was so much worry. For her. Only for her.

How was that possible too with the curse intact? He should be blind and they both should not be able to feel any of this. Although, Bas always had. That was an extra cruelty Clodia had baked into the curse that separated them before she'd almost managed to steal Julianna's power.

She was not supposed to remember Bas, but he would always remember her. He would remember what they were to each other. He would have the agony of loving her but never having that love returned. For thousands of years.

Horrific. Tragic.

And yet he'd never faltered. Never tried to leave her. Never given up hope. Because if he had ... if he had ... this would never have happened.

He would never have broken the curse.

That was the only way this could have happened. He'd broken the curse.

She lifted her hand and cupped his face, thumb brushing over his beautiful lips, and stared into those amazing eyes. "You did this. You broke it. You broke the curse."

"I ... I ..." He shook his head slowly. "I didn't. I didn't think the curse could be broken until the anniversary of the day on which it was cast."

She nodded. She knew that. The knowledge had always been there, just not accessible to her until now. She took in a deep breath, trying to take it in. She let the breath out slowly and said as evenly as she could, "And yet, it is gone. I can remember. Everything. And you ... you are no longer a cat familiar during the day. And you can see."

His hand lifted to touch next to his eyes. "I can see you with my own eyes."

"Your beautiful eyes."

He smiled gently at her. "I can stare into your beautiful eyes from now until the end of me."

She hissed out a pained breath as she cupped his face. "Don't even think that let alone say the words aloud. You cannot ever end."

"I can. But not for a very long time unless a God or Goddess kills me. And if we get your powers back, because they are Goddess-gifted, they will give you the same kind of longevity."

"But how can we get them back when Clodia has had them all this time?"

He shook his head. "She never got them. Something went awry. I saw it happen as I lay on the ground in my cat form, almost unconscious. The powers didn't go into her. They turned on her instead and stole her life from her."

"She died?"

"She did. Not long after she buried you alive."

"Good."

"Yes." His smile was as satisfied as hers felt, his fingers brushing over her cheek. "So if we can find out what happened to your powers and get them back to you, we can be together for whatever length of time our immortality gives us."

"That sounds good to me." She breathed in deeply, taking in the wonderful scent of him. She wanted to bathe in that scent, to cover herself in it so that she would never be without it again. Never not understand the significance and wonder of it again. But there was something she needed to say before she could find a way to do that. Because he was right. She needed her power if they were to have their forever after. The curse wasn't truly broken until they had that.

"What is it?"

She brushed her thumb over his lips again, loving the soft, warmth of them against her skin. "I want my forever with you."

"That is my greatest wish too."

She nodded. She knew it was. "So how are we to get my powers back? Can you just do some sort of spell to summon them?"

"No. I'm afraid it is not that simple. And even if it was, that is not in my power to do. I am a cupid – powers I got from my father – and a healer witch – powers I got from my mother." He flexed his hand and a golden glow appeared there. A fast puff of breath left his lips. "I have that back."

She grasped his hand and stared at the golden glow. "It's not hurting me."

"I know. Your magical allergy was part of the curse too."

She nodded. She knew that. That knowledge had been at the back of her mind just like everything else about this had been, but now it was all in the front of it. She supposed that was going to happen a lot now as memories came back to her. She was kind of glad she wasn't getting all the memories at once. The ones that had already come back to her had almost taken her down with the horror of them.

But not all of them were full of horror. Just those last months after Clodia had caught them and trapped them until she could do what she wanted to do. Which was after the baby was born. Because she wanted the power of the new born cupid as well.

She gasped as memory of the child came back into her thoughts. "What happened to our son?"

Bas broke her gaze, looking down at their cupped hands. "I do not know. He was gone when I came to. I tried to search for him but the curse wouldn't let me. I've done all the research I could think of to try to find out what happened to him, but have never discovered anything. He just disappeared. Your young cousin and fellow Vestal Virgin, Esta, told me that a God had arrived that night and took him but she had no idea who it was or where he took him. She was so grief stricken at your loss and shocked over what had happened, but thankfully that night she had the wherewithal to pick up my weak cat form and took me to the Stevius family home and looked after me. She bound me to the Stevius line with her powers to ensure I would always have a place with them and I have been with her family – your family – ever since."

"Oh Bas." She cupped his face. "I don't know what to say. You've been trapped by the curse all these years, knowing who you are and what we were to each other, looking for our son and unable to tell anyone – including me and all the other versions of me I've been. I can't imagine ..." She shook her head, tears forming in her eyes. "I can't imagine what you've suffered."

"You've suffered too. All those years never being able to be your true self. Your full self. Never able to remember. Never able to fully love or accept love. Never having your powers in a family with tremendous power. I have watched over and over as you've suffered from what became not just a lack of power, but an increasingly violent allergy to magic's very presence."

Tears were pouring down her face as she dropped her hands to his chest, clenching against his warm skin. "That's nothing in comparison to what you've suffered. I couldn't remember from life to life, so I took none of that agony with me."

It was his turn to cup her face, his thumbs brushing her tears. "You may not have remembered it, but the curse made sure it marked your soul. So often, you were barely even you. So quick to mistrust. So distant from everyone around you. There were incarnations where I worried that it was damaging your soul so much that I would never get you back."

"But you got me back. You got me back." Her hands slid up to cup his face too and she leaned up to kiss him lightly. "And this time, I'm never letting you go."

"Me either. I will never let you go again."

"You never did let me go. You stayed all this time despite what it did to you. If I didn't already love you so much, I would love you simply for that." She kissed him again, her lips pressing a little harder, a little more desperately, but before he could meet her with any enthusiasm, she pulled back to look up into his passion-filled gaze. "We have to find him, Bas. I can't rest until I know what happened to our son."

"We won't. I'm so sorry I'm not able to tell you. That I didn't find him."

"We'll find him together."

"Yes. We'll find him together."

She smiled up at him. "Do you have any idea where we should start?"

He stared down at her for long moments. She reached up to touch his face, feeling the sadness he felt because he didn't have better news for her.

He nuzzled into her touch and smiled softly. "Maybe Tamuel will be able to help us."

"Tamuel?"

"The cupid who has been helping me. He's the one who came up with the idea to do the Christmas wish that broke the curse."

"A Christmas wish?"

"Yes. Although, we never imagined it would break the curse. Tamuel simply thought that a Christmas wish would help to give you back your Christmas Spirit and break us both out of the depression we were falling into – you particularly."

"I remember," she said wonderingly. She did remember. She'd been lying on the bed, such hopelessness filling her she could barely move and the two of them had come in – although she couldn't see Tamuel for some reason. Despite Bas' obvious worry, they had made a wish.

And everything had changed.

"That disembodied voice ... he was Tamuel?"

Bas nodded. "He's been helping me for a while now to find a way to break the curse. Neither of us expected it to work like this. It wasn't supposed to work like this." He frowned and shook his head a little. "I'm not sure why it did."

"But it did."

His smile flashed back into place. "Yes, it did. We finally found our way back to each other and we don't have to wait until Valentine's Eve to do it."

"Valentine's Eve? Why is that significant?"

"Well, thanks to your Grandmama and her research into curses, we found out that the only way to break a curse when the curse creator isn't there to break it was to do so at the exact same hour, date and place where they were originally cast, with the same incantation. The problem with curses as ancient as ours is that the way we mark time has changed so significantly that it can be difficult to track down the exact hour and date. But your grandmama helped us to figure out our curse was cast on Valentine's Eve at midnight."

"That's great."

"Yes, it is. Except ..." He rubbed his brow and frowned. "The problem is, we never could figure out the exact place. Something about the curse ensured I couldn't remember. And most of what we knew as *Roma* is now in ruins, so even if I go there, I'm unlikely to be able to piece it together from visual cues."

"It was in the temple garden." She frowned deeply, trying to bring up the painful memories. Julianna had been blindfolded on the journey there and when Clodia had finally taken the blindfold off, it had been dark and she was in labour and she really hadn't taken note of her surroundings. All she could think of was fears for the child she was birthing and grief over what was being torn from her. "I'm sorry. I can't remember anything more beyond that."

He shook his head. "Don't be sorry. We had hope. Tamuel has been tracking down Esta's diary which was lost many centuries ago. It is out there though and we know she wrote everything down from that night. And we also hoped that putting the diary in front of you would start to bring memories back. Memories you would need to help us break the curse."

"But we don't need it now."

He brushed his fingers over her cheeks and smiled down at her in a way that made her stomach curl. "No," he said softly. "We don't."

They stood there, smiling at each other for long moments, but slowly, the smiles faded until she whispered. "We have to find him. Our son."

"We will. Tamuel will help us."

"How do we contact him?"

"I'll try to call him through the cupid network. But if I can't get him that way, I have no doubt he'll be back soon. He won't be able to stop himself from coming back and checking on how we're going. It was his wish too, that we break the curse."

"I want to thank him. Is there anything I can do?"

He looked down at her consideringly. "Enjoy this Christmas. It was a bit strange given he's a cupid and doesn't share in the Christian mythology and traditions, but he was rather upset that we didn't have our usual Christmas decorations up and glowing. It was what tipped him off to things being so bad – that and the fact our depression was starting to seep into the ley-lines under the library – and made him suggest the wish."

"Oh. It's Christmas!" She spun around, hands clasped. "I'd completely forgotten. Or just didn't care. Why didn't I care?"

"You were depressed. So was I for that matter."

"Oh." She turned back to him, frowning. "How long until Christmas?"

"Just under two weeks now."

"Two weeks! We've barely got enough time to do every-thing. You'll help me, right?"

"Of course."

"I'm sure Grandmama will be happy to help by putting up decorations with her magic as she usually does." She clapped her hands together. "And I won't have to leave the house this time when she does! I might not have my magic back, but not being allergic to other people's magic is almost as good." She frowned a little as a thought hit her. "I think that more than anything else was pushing me into depression. Being non-magical in a family of strong witches is bad enough. Being allergic to magic was really a step too far."

"Clodia was diabolical with her curse."

"She was indeed." She clapped her hands together

again, this time in a decisive 'let's get down to work' kind of way. "So, Christmas. We need to get the decorations out and then you and I should go and pick us some Christmas trees from the farm. And while we're out, Grandmama can start on decorating the areas I can't reach by ladder. Are you up for decorating and baking duty?"

"Sure am. I've missed the smell of baking and spices."

She wondered if her eyes were twinkling with delight in the same way his were. "Me too. The smell of the fruit cakes, gingerbread and shortbread filling the house always makes me happy. I don't know why I didn't want to do it this year."

"It doesn't matter," he said, brushing her hair back from her face and hooking it over her ear – by the Goddess she enjoyed more than words could express the freedom to be able to accept such a simple caress. He seemed to enjoy it too, his love and delight shining from his eyes as he stared into hers and said, "All that matters is we are both up for all the baking and decorating now. If we work non-stop for the next few days, I think we can get this done."

"Don't forget the present buying too."

"How could I forget that!"

"And I want to do something for all those in need and doing it hard. More than I ever have before."

"Of course you do."

"We've got so much to do. How will we get it all done?"

"Don't worry. We'll get it done. Operation Christmas in less than two weeks is underway." He held his hand up for her to high-five.

She grinned widely at him and slapped her hand against his. "Let's get Christmassy!"

CHAPTER

TEN

Rudolph landed with a thump that had Tam's teeth snapping together so hard it made his jaw ache.

"Woohoo!" Gary yelled, seeming to enjoy the roughness of the ride they'd just endured.

Tam rather thought he might hurl. Or would have if the ride hadn't ended when it did. He swallowed hard, rubbing at his sore jaw and grumbled, "You're a crazy arse, Gary."

"Thanks, Tamuel. I try my best to be. Keeps things lively up here in the Pole."

Tam made a huffing, unamused sound. "Things a bit boring for you are they? Santa not keeping you busy enough?"

"Ptoue. Ptoue," Gary said, spitting sideways over raised fingers like a Greek Grandma warding off the evil eye. "Don't even put that thought out there. Santa might get an idea he needs to become a greater taskmaster than he already is to take more of the weight off his shoulders. It's not like Mrs Claus isn't constantly on his back about the fact he has no down time. Especially at this time of the year."

"You don't want to help your boss as much as you possibly can? I thought that was the elf raison d'être."

"Of course it is. And of course we do. But we're already more than busy, thank you very much. Especially this one handsome elf you see before you. I am Santa's right-hand elf after all. But young elves need to blow off steam just as surely as the reindeer do, and I really don't need more responsibility thrust on my young shoulders right now. I don't want to be my father – he died way too young because he was all work and no play."

"I'm sorry to hear that," Tam said, his face falling into lines of empathy. He really did feel empathy for anyone who didn't get to spend enough time with their father or mother – up until recently, he'd never got to spend time with his, and to make matters worse, they didn't even know he was their son, nor could they until he was certain the curse was broken and Jules' magic was back where it was supposed to be. Inside of her. "Did you not get to know him very well? Did he die when you were a young elf?"

Gary turned to stare at him over his shoulder. "I was a bit young, only 1000 when he passed. He was a youthful 10,000." He shook his head sadly and swiped at his eye. "Way too young."

"Uh, yeah. Sounds like it." Tam knew elves were long-lived, but he kind of thought that ten thousand equated to about 70 or 80 in human years, so not that young by any stretch of the imagination. Not old either, but not unexpected that someone that age might pass away. And as for Gary being 1000 at the time of his father's death – well, that was like being a late teen in human years. So he certainly wasn't young and had got to spend significant time with his father. Certainly far more time than Tam had ever got to spend with his.

"Ah crapsticks," Gary said on an explosion of breath.

"What?" Tam asked, surprised to hear the swear word on the mouth of an elf.

"Time is going all kaflooey," he said, waving his arm around. "It's taken us far longer to get here than it should have. It's affecting Santa worse than I thought it was if he's made time go all wibbly wobbly again."

"How can you tell what time it is?" Tam asked, looking around at the dark landscape – permanently so at this time of year. "I can't see a timepiece."

"I'm an elf. I don't need a timepiece," Gary said in a tone that sounded distinctly ominous. Then he barked, "Brace yourself."

"For what?" Tam asked but then got hit with the icy chill of the North Pole as Rudolph dropped the travel shield he'd raised when flying through the portal. Wind and snow blasted Tam in the face – he rather thought the sensation must be like that treatment women paid thousands of dollars for where they got the top layer of their skin blasted off. It *hurt!* Why on earth would anyone do this to them- selves purposefully let alone pay all that money for it?

Spluttering, he wiped what felt like centimetres of snow off his cheeks, chin and brow. "Thanks for the warning."

"What are you talking about? I did warn you."

"The second before it was about to happen. I had no time to protect myself."

"That's not my problem. My problem was to bring you here. I've done that. Now off you hop and in you go."

"Go in whe—!" Rudolph reared. "Agh!" Tam went tumbling off the reindeer's back, rolling across the snow and in through a door that suddenly appeared as if out of nowhere. The hard, cold pack of snow changed to the warm-hardness of wood as he continued to roll across the room he was now in until he abruptly stopped, crashing into something big and black and rubbery.

"Ho-ho-ho! That was quite the entry, my young cupid friend."

Tam looked up and up and up, past the black boots, the red-clad legs, the washboard stomach shown off in a skin-tight red t-shirt. Rather than the jolly fat man most people thought of as Santa, the man himself was built like Adonis with a snowy-white beard that hung halfway down a broad chest and sparkling light blue eyes set in a face that was all chiseled jaw and cheekbones, and straight sharp nose that would have made Byron weep with longing.

Tam sucked in his breath. He'd forgotten just how Godsdamned hot Saint Nicholas really was. If he was like any other cupid who liked to experiment sexually and hadn't fallen hot and hard for a female witch centuries ago, a love he had never ever gotten over, he really would have had a big hard-on for good old Saint Nick. Not that he'd have any luck with him. Since meeting Merry Claus, Nick had become a one-woman man.

"Are you okay, son? Cat got your tongue?" Santa ho-ho-hoed down at him again before reaching down with his large, masculine hand and gripped Tam under the shoulder, hauling him up. "There. Is that better? Not so topsy-turvy."

Tam nodded. "Thanks." It did help that he was no longer looking up Santa's long, muscled length – not to mention he was no longer trying not to stare at the rather large package nestled in Santa's far too tight red pants. A package that was most likely responsible for the smile that was always on Merry Claus' face in every painting he'd ever seen of them together. He'd never really noticed it before – probably because he wasn't looking, but most particularly because he'd never looked up at Santa from his feet region before. Their few meetings had been face to face and on their feet – thank the Gods because it wasn't something that could be easily forgotten and Tam really didn't need to be carrying that visual around with him all these years.

Actually, the problem was that Tam didn't quite know where to look now he'd seen it. It was like it had its own gravitational force, pulling his attention back to it. To try to fight that pull, Tam studiously looked around the room. "Nice chair," he said, nodding at the space-aged looking leather contraption nestled in the corner by the window.

Nick beamed. "Ah, yes. It's where I like to do my Christmas Wish and Christmas Spirit work from. It's an original Flöghstrom."

"IKEA?"

"No-ho-ho-ho," Nick chuckled. "Flöghstrom is a new Icelandic furniture designer I discovered. He uses all recycled timber and sustainable leather and makes things to specific order to suit the size of the client. It's the most comfortable chair I've ever had the pleasure of sitting in – and I've had some wonderful chairs." His blue-blue eyes sparkled with all the memories of chairs he'd owned over the years.

For just a moment, Tam felt a little jealous of such memories. Being a cupid, for most of his life he had never settled in one spot long enough to truly get to know a piece of furniture or for the furniture to truly get to know him. Even now with the pocket universe he'd created for his private study getaway where he could plan and scheme without any God or Goddess, or overly-curious Grandfather, looking over his shoulder and figuring out what he was doing he hadn't really found the kind of furniture that made him sigh happily just to think of sitting in it. He had one old big black leather winged armchair which was promising, but so far he hadn't really had enough time to sit in it and make it shape to his bones. He was still too busy running around trying to pretend he wasn't doing what he was doing.

Because he wasn't supposed to be wasting his time on breaking a curse none of his pantheon considered important enough to break. Of course, his research had suggested something else entirely, but he wasn't going to waste his time taking that research to any of them and trying to change their minds because exercises in futility were not the hill he wanted to break himself on. Besides, this was something he needed to do for himself. And his mum and dad. They all deserved more.

They all deserved to be with each other.

"Nick, is he here yet ... ah, there you are you rascally boy."

Before he had time to even register her presence, Merry Claus had swept him up into her arms and had him in the kind of motherly hug he'd longed to have experience of when he was a boy. Well, it would be a motherly hug if not for the fact she'd pulled his head down to rest on her Jessica Rabbit style breasts that were currently encased in a very tight, low cut, lace-ruffled red velvet dress with twinkling lights blinking on and off all over it.

He managed to extricate himself as politely as possible, aware that Nick was eyeballing him.

Usually very congenial, Nick could suddenly be unreasonably jealous of the particular kind of attention that was often given to his rather luscious wife. The comparison with Jessica Rabbit was no exaggeration – she had smouldering curves, large brown eyes, luscious red lips, auburn hair that fell in loose waves around her shoulders and a husky voice that would give Roger Rabbit's wife a run for her money. Except of course, Jessica Rabbit was a cartoon and Merry Claus was very, very real and very, very sexy and very, very friendly. Sometimes too friendly according to Nick.

Not that he didn't trust his wife, he'd assured Tam one time. No, it was that he didn't trust other men, women and non-binaries to not react to her very overt sexuality and smouldering ways. It was one of the reasons he worked with elves – her charms didn't work on them in the same way. They only saw her as a cuddly, mother-type they loved, like they'd love their favourite Nanna. It was why she was seen as a cuddly grandmother type by the world – because the paintings the elves did of her, the ones that had got out into the world, always pictured her as such and she was too kind to make them redo those paintings and paint her as she truly was.

Santa of course had encouraged them to continue painting her in this way for anything that went outside the home.

He glanced over at Nick and was relieved to see that he was smiling at his wife and Tam. Whew. He'd obviously managed to extricate himself from a Merry greeting before things got truly awkward. Puffing out a breath and stepping away from Merry – who immediately went over to Nick and tucked herself into his strapping side – he swung his arms back and forth, rocking on his heels. "Well," he said after a moment when they did nothing but look back at him.

"Well," Nick said.

"Umm, yes ... well?" Tam said, starting to feel not a little awkward again. He couldn't help but notice Merry was running her hand over her husband's chest in a way that was more appropriate for the bedroom than the living room.

"Well, well, well," Merry giggled huskily. "Three holes in the ground."

"Ho-ho-ho!" Nick chortled. "Good one my love."

She beamed up at him and he leaned down and kissed her soundly – oh Gods, was that a bit of tongue? He didn't need to see that.

But it seemed he was seeing that – and so much more. What started as a peck had turned into something far more passionate before he could even think to turn away. Urgh yuck. There was definitely massive amounts of tongue going on between Nick and Merry. And Merry's hand was making its way down from Nick's expansive chest, across his stomach and to his—

No-no-no!

Turning away, Tam tried to pretend he was anywhere but here. Should he leave? He'd only just arrived and still didn't know what Nick had wanted him here for. And the only place to go was out the door he'd just come in. He didn't want to go out there because he truly wasn't dressed for the kind of cold you found up here at the North Pole at this time of year – he had one of his lightweight summer suits on in deference to the Australian climate where he'd been spending most of his time recently. And he couldn't rely on his increasingly fritzing magic to be able to use it to call some warmer clothing to him.

Maybe he could make a quick retreat through the door Merry had come through which led to the main house that was truly her domain. Although, from memory, if he stepped through that door, he'd be swamped by elves over-eager to ensure he looked Christmassy enough for Merry's liking. Not to mention he was likely to be blinded by all the twinkle lights and excess of colour that Santa's wifey loved so much. It was because of her that the entire Christmas decoration industry truly started. Many of her designs now graced the homes of people all over the world. Although, the red, gold and silver penis decorations with the light-up testicles had thankfully never caught on in the way she'd hoped. He'd never forgotten the last time he'd been here and had been invited for dinner and had walked into the dining room to be greeted by merrily blinking and flashing coloured penises in the Christmas trees that sat in each corner of the room all year round, not to mention the rather large phallus lights that sat in pride of place down the centre of the table and changed colour through the spectrum.

It had been really difficult to swallow down anything that night. Phalluses might have been all the rage for decorations in ancient Roman times, but they really weren't something he wanted to see while eating his dinner.

He began to whistle and turned to look out the window just in time to see the herd of reindeer flying in formation, Rudolph's red nose flashing vibrantly at their lead.

"Have you told him yet?" Gary asked as he bustled in the door in a flurry of snow and a blast of cold wind.

Tam wrapped his arms around himself and edged closer to the fire, uncomfortably aware that Gary's intrusion hadn't done anything to stop Nick and Merry from trying to swallow each other's tongues while grinding against each other like two horny teenagers at a rave.

Tam coughed and studiously looked anywhere but at Santa and his wife – which meant he wasn't looking at Gary who was currently standing right in front of his bosses, hands on his hips, although, he realised he could see them quite well in the window as Gary said petulantly, "Oh come on, you two! I thought you weren't going to give into this. It's not like you don't know what's going on."

In the window reflection Tam saw Merry wave her hand dismissively at Gary as she continued to grind against her hubby and kiss him like there was no tomorrow.

"No. I'm not going to go away." Gary stamped his foot. "If you don't stop right now, I'm going to go and get Rudolph and he'll spark you apart. You won't like that."

Merry held up one finger – and not in a 'wait a minute' kind of way.

Gary mirrored her middle finger action before turning and racing across to the window. He quickly pulled it open – letting in a gust of cold and snow – and yelled out, "Rudolph! They're at it again!"

There was a slurping popping sound and then, "Shut that window you little spoilsport," Merry snapped.

Tam glanced around to see she had pulled away from her hubby, her red lipstick smeared across her mouth and chin – and Santa's. He wished he hadn't looked though – Merry was busy reseating her large bosom in her tight dress as Santa was adjusting himself in his red pants. Tam spun back around to face the window before his gaze could get stuck on the massive stiffy in Santa's pants.

He really wished there was a way you could take your eyeballs out and wash them. There were so many things he wished he hadn't seen – and they had all happened within the last ten minutes!

Gary yelled out the window, "Don't worry about it Rudi. They're behaving themselves now." Then he slammed the window shut – thank the Gods because Tam's teeth had begun to chatter – and turned to glare at the horny couple. "Honestly, I thought I told you both to stay away from each other while this is going on."

"I needed to be in on this," Merry said. "You can't keep me out of it, you little martinet."

"Call me all the names you like, you big horn bag, but you know I'm right because you agreed to it."

Merry pouted. "Well, I'm not going anywhere now."

"Then you," he pointed at Merry, "go over to that side of the room and you," pointing at Santa, "go over to that side. Tam and I will stand in the middle."

"Do we have to?" Tam asked, teeth still chattering. He really didn't want to move away from the fire.

Gary glared at him and Tam sighed and moved into the middle of the room. He really should be wondering what the Hells was going on between them all – he knew Nick and Merry were a very loved-up couple, but what he'd just witnessed was unusual even for them as far as he was aware. And if what Gary was saying could be taken at face value, his supposition was right. He should be worried except ... he was way too cold to care about anything until he'd warmed up a little.

"Can you stop that?" Gary said to him as the elf came and stood next to him.

Tam looked down at him, brow raised. "St-st-st-stop wh-wh-what?"

"That teeth chattering," Gary said, nose wrinkled like he'd smelled dog poop. "It's really grating on my nerves."

"I-I-I-I-m c-c-c-c-c-cold."

"Oh for fuck sake," he growled. Then turning toward the internal door, he bellowed, "Southerner's a big wuss. Turn up the heat and bring in the hot chocolates."

Another elf poked her head through the door. "Peppermint stick in yours, sir?"

"Of course."

"I wouldn't mind a peppermint stick," Santa said.

"Me too."

"You can have a peppermint stick if you promise to behave for the rest of the day. I'm sick of having to break the two of you apart. I swear if I have to see your boobs again, Merry and your massive eggplant again, Nick, then I'm going to cry sexual harassment and report you to the HR department."

"You are the HR department," Merry pointed out.

"Well, I'll report you to myself. And believe me," he said, wagging his finger at them. "I won't let you off easy."

Merry and Santa shared a look and then nodded. "Fine," Merry said. "We promise to behave."

Gary looked at Santa.

"I promise too," Santa said seriously, holding up his hands in a Scout's honour hand signal.

"And after this meeting, once our plan is in place, you will return to your side of the house, Merry. And you will stay in this room, Santa, until we're ready to leave."

They were going somewhere?

"Can I keep cooking the treats?" Merry asked before Tam could ask the question.

"Of course. It will keep you busy. And Santa, after we have taken care of this and have returned, you will need to stay in here until we are completely certain all the energies have settled."

Santa nodded. "Of course. I would be in here anyway keeping the Christmas Spirit on the straight and narrow."

"Yes, but unlike usual, you won't be able to leave this room until we're certain and Merry can't come in. The elves will have to completely take care of you."

"Very well."

He turned and glared at Merry until she sighed and nodded too.

"Good." Gary sighed loudly, then turned toward the elf who still had her head poked around the door. "Peppermint sticks all around, Sandy."

"Good-o, sir. Anything to eat?"

He looked at the others, brows raised.

"I wouldn't mind some raisin toast," Santa said.

"Raisin toast all round too. And don't skimp on the butter," Gary said.

"Of course not, sir. It will be dripping off. I'll make sure of it myself."

"Lovely."

The elf – Sandy – disappeared back through the door and silence fell on the room, only broken by the crackling of the fire, which had suddenly grown. In fact, the entire fireplace had increased in size and now took up a third of the wall it stood in. The heat radiating from it washed over Tam in a warming wave that had him sighing in relief. In moments his teeth had stopped chattering and he was able to drop his hands from hugging around his body and rubbing his arms.

He now felt capable of asking about why he'd been brought here and what the Hells they'd all been talking about. But before he could open his mouth, Gary said abruptly. "Now the cupid is toasty warm, how about we get to why you sent me out at the busiest time of the year to fetch him."

ELEVEN

Santa looked at Merry, his eyebrows raised.

"Don't look at me like that, my love. This is your to-do." She raised her hands. "I'm not in charge of the wish department no matter how often I've told you it might be better if I was."

Santa sighed. "If I've told you once, I've told you a million-trillion times, my love, only I can grant Christmas wishes because only I am Santa."

"And I've told you a million-trillion and one times, my love, that that is a load of centuries old misogynistic – not to mention – narcissistic thinking wrapped up in fresh reindeer manure. I've been your wife for centuries and I have worked with you on your calling before we even got together. I have as much Christmas Spirit as you do and my magic is only getting stronger as each year passes. I am perfectly capable of taking some of the load off your shoulders in granting Christmas wishes – in actual fact, I am probably better suited to granting them at this time when your energies are better given over to your greater calling of spreading Christmas Spirit."

"And we probably wouldn't be in this mess if she was in charge of it because her attention wouldn't have been split across too many concerns," Gary grumbled, folding his arms in front of his chest. "Merry also wouldn't have made the gargantuan mistake of granting a wish where such a powerful curse was involved." He squared his jaw as Santa turned to glare at him, uncrossing his arms to point an accusing finger at his boss. "And don't get all huffy with me as if this is the first time we've had this discussion. You know very well that I agree with your missus and always have. You know the elves stance on you continuing to take too much upon yourself. You're running yourself ragged, especially now with the world in the state that it's in needing more of your energy than ever before to keep the Christmas Spirit at acceptable levels year round. It was the fact your mind was on too many different things that this wish was granted in the first place. And now look at what's happened."

Tam had been watching and listening with great interest but now his teeth had stopped chattering and he no longer needed to hug himself and jig up and down on the spot for warmth, he decided to ask one of the many questions their very interesting conversation was raising in his head. "Umm, are you talking about *my* Christmas wish."

Gary nodded. "Uh-huh. Yours and the other cupid's."

"Bastien."

"That's the one."

"Such a lovely cupid," Santa said jovially, his face splitting into a wide smile before it fell into deep frown lines. "Such a terrible thing that happened to him. And to that lovely Julianna Stevius. If I'd been alive back then and had my powers, I would not have allowed such a travesty to take place. Clodia would have well and truly been on my naughty list long before she cast her curse. She would have been punished for preying on the power of those who were supposed to be under her care for all those years." He shook his head sadly. "When I came into my powers centuries later and became aware of the reincarnated lives of that poor Vestal Virgin witch and the curse that affected her and her cupid love – Sebastio as he was called back then – I couldn't help but watch over them as much as I could through the centuries. I admired Bastien – as he's known now – and the reincarnations of Julianna so very much for not becoming cold and embittered. I have to hope that some of the Christmas Spirit and goodwill I sent their way had some influence on that." He preened a little. "But I can't take too much credit for what an astonishing woman this incarnation has grown into. So accomplished despite her ever-growing magical disability. I have very much enjoyed watching her grow year after year, with Bastien such a stalwart companion at her side. But even so, I felt sorry that I could do nothing to help him as he pined for her, unable to ever express it."

"We know the story, my love," Merry said, shaking her head at him. "You don't need to tell us all about it again. We've been watching with you for centuries."

Tam shook his head, still trying to take in all that had been said. "You've been watching them?"

Santa nodded at Tam. "Of course. Such a tragedy and yet we couldn't make ourselves look away."

"Car crash viewing is what it's called," Gary said grumpily.

"Well, I don't particularly like that analogy," Santa said, frowning at Gary now. "But I suppose it does kind of explain the fascination we have all had with Julianna and Bastien's story as it's unfolded over the centuries. And then when you became involved, my boy!" Santa said, gesturing at Tam. "Wo-ho-ho! Well, it's become a roller-coaster of excitement for us to watch as you navigated dealing with both Violetta in one persona and Bastien in another, all while hiding yourself from Jules. What a performance!"

"Uh, thanks?" Tam said, utterly confused and bemused.

"My pleasure," Santa beamed.

"But ... why didn't you mention this to me before on the occasions I've caught up with you."

"Didn't see the point," Santa said. "There wasn't anything I could do to help other than to send you all as much positive energy as possible. I also helped Jules enjoy her Christmases given she couldn't participate in her coven's Yule celebrations, and made certain her family were happy to help."

"So what changed now?"

"Well, you made your wish," he said proudly, smile widening. "So I grabbed the opportunity to do something more just as I've been wishing to do this many y ..." His words petered out as Santa seemed to notice the look his wife was aiming at him. "Well ... um ... yes," he said, coughing to clear his throat as he schooled his features into something more solemn. "As I said, having watched you all for some time, I was invested in your stories and wanted to help. And I have succeeded every year until this one. It was so horrible to watch her going into such a funk, with Bas following her down that dark path too. It was one of the reasons I answered your Christmas wish so readily."

"Which you shouldn't have done," Merry said tightly.

"Word, sister," Gary said solemnly.

"Don't start on me again," Santa said grumpily. "You know I hate it when you gang up on me like this."

"We do it because you need bringing down a peg or

two, my love," Merry said. "You do get carried away with your jolly self at times, thinking you can do more than you should to help people. You know, you can't fix all the world's ills. That's not your job."

"Well, it is kind of my job."

"Your job is creating Christmas Spirit that lasts across the year so that other people can join in on doing the job of making the world a better place. It is not to actually get hands on and make the world a better place yourself, one person – or couple as the case may be – at a time."

"I don't know why you get those two things confused," Gary chimed in. "It's as clear as clear can be in the Saint Nicholas Charter, as written by the Fairy of Good Tidings." He turned to Tam, explaining, "It was the Fairy of Good Tidings who gave him the job and boosted his magic to the extent where it could spread across the world and not just in the closer Eastern European countries near his original home in Myra where this all began."

"Why do you always have to throw that bloody Charter in my face?" Santa asked grumpily.

"Because I was the one who wrote it. My mother, that very same Fairy of Good Tidings who gave you the job, put me in charge of writing it and making sure you stuck to it – even she knew your generous nature might make you want to do more than you should or could. That's why she insisted on writing down the position description and the rules by which you need to be bound. It's as much to safe-guard your wellbeing as ensure the world gets what she knew it needed because she knew she was not going to be around forever."

He turned to Tam again, gesturing with his hand at the painting on the wall next to the window – one of Odin as the Yule Father. "She needed to ensure that what Odin started during the Wild Hunt as the Yule Father was continued in the world even while worship of Odin and his pantheon waned. She loved Odin so much and wanted his legacy of knowledge, wisdom and goodness to live on in some way, especially after his troublesome children, and the threat of Ragnarök, pushed his more excellent qualities from the general consciousness. She just couldn't stand the thought that knowledge of who he truly was would die with her. That's why she was so thrilled when Saint Nicholas came along and did things very similar to what Odin did at Yule – but all year around. She'd waited so long and then there he was, doing good deeds that created magical energy that encouraged charity and good deeds in others even through the hardship of the fourth century. She was so happy. She jumped on the challenge of making him more. And she did it. Because Santa Claus has become legend the world over. She would be so proud. So happy." Gary swiped at his eyes and sniffled.

"She was an amazing woman, Gary," Merry said softly.

"That she was." He took a deep, shuddering breath before aiming a steely look at Santa. "And she'd be very upset if she found out about what you've done in granting this Christmas wish when you knew bloody-well that you shouldn't do it."

Tam was trying desperately to wrap his head around everything they had just said and were now saying – his head was still spinning somewhat from the wild ride here. But when Gary mentioned the Christmas wish once again – and come to think of it, Merry had mentioned the wish in the same negative context too – his focus arrowed in on that and he couldn't help but blurting out, "What do you mean you shouldn't have granted my Christmas wish?"

All three of them turned to him, surprise clearly on their

faces as if they'd forgotten he was there. Merry was the first to recover though, because she quickly lost the look of surprise and replaced it with one of sympathy – the kind of sympathy that made his stomach curl nastily rather than giving him the warm fuzzies.

"Oh, dear boy. Yes, the granting of your Christmas wish was a terrible mistake."

"But ... but why? It broke the curse. The one that has made Bas and Jules' lives such a misery. Particularly lately. Their depression was seeping out of the house and into the ley-lines under it and had started to affect other magical creatures. Before long, it would have affected the humans too. Granting that Christmas wish saved more than Bas and Jules – it possibly saved the world from a depression greater than any it had ever been through in the past. You know very well that the other times ley-lines have been so negatively affected it allowed great evil to rise, most recently in the likes of Hitler and Pol Pot and Duke Leo. Not to mention negatively affected ley-lines have caused most of the wars that have ever been. Surely that is something Santa should be interested in – stopping that kind of negativity from giving rise to that kind of evil again, especially given it is already so close to the surface with what is going on in the world? Surely that is a wish he would naturally want to grant? For the good of Christmas. For the good of Peoplekind."

Santa coughed awkwardly. "Yes, well, one would think that. And this Santa did think that at the time ... but you see, it seems that I was perhaps mistaken?" He pulled a face at his wife and head elf.

"There is no perhaps about it, Nick," Gary said acerbically. "You absolutely, definitely shouldn't have granted that wish."

"But if he hadn't granted it, it would have affected the world," Tam argued again, brow furrowing even harder as confusion and anger warred for ascendancy inside of him.

"Yes ... and we would have worked some particularly difficult Christmas magic to ensure the impact of their depression wasn't pushed out into the world but remained only around Stevens House," Merry said. "All of us were preparing for such a working and then my beloved went and granted your wish and all of that preparation went for nought."

"That's a good thing, surely?" Tam said, shaking his head. "Now you can expend all that magic on other, better things."

Gary snorted. "Yeah, one would think that, but no."

"What do you mean?" Tam asked.

"Magic is being expended that's for certain, although I wouldn't say it was on better things." He eyed Santa and Merry then pointed a stern finger at them as they looked like they were about to move towards each other. "Uh-uh-uh. Don't you move from those spots." He waved his hand and a surge of magic shoved through the room, splitting in two to create two clear bubbles which fled towards Santa and Merry.

"Gary, don't you—" Santa began as Merry shrieked and tried to move backwards. But it didn't help. The bubbles slammed into them, encapsulated them and caught them inside – one in each bubble which hovered above the ground on opposite sides of the room.

"Gary!" Santa shouted, his voice echoing softly from inside his bubble. "Let me out of here now!"

"No." Gary crossed his arms.

"I can't believe you snow-globed us!" Merry shrieked as she banged against the globe, her hands making a dull thud against what appeared to be incredibly strong glass or Perspex.

"Be thankful I didn't call in Rudolph to spark you. Or add the snow to the globe," Gary said ominously. "I warned you the moment it began to happen that if you couldn't keep it in your pants and stay away from each other, I would make sure you did." He waggled his finger between them. "You two just gave me no choice."

"Umm, aren't you worried about what they'll do to you when you let them out?" Tam asked as he moved surreptitiously further away from Gary – if he could do that to Santa and Merry, Tam was a bit worried about what the elf might do to him.

Gary shrugged. "I'm more worried about what would happen if I didn't safeguard against the rebound of the curse being broken by your wish being granted."

"I don't know what the big deal is. The curse was broken by my wish – so what?"

TWELVE

Gary pulled a 'what the fuck man?' face at him. "What do you mean so what? There is no 'so what's about this. The upshot of you breaking the curse with the wish has not been pretty. The impact of it is certain to do more damage than what your parents' depression would have done to the world."

"Why? I don't understand why you're so worried."

"Isn't it obvious?" Gary said, gesturing between Santa and Merry who were glaring angrily at the elf as they floated within their respective globes.

Tam squeezed his eyes shut for a moment, trying desperately to make sense out of everything that had been said since he'd been dumped in this room, but he couldn't seem to string together sense from any of it. Shaking his head, he opened his eyes to see all three of them frowning at him. "What? Why are you looking at me like that?"

"Because we need you to reverse your wish," Gary said.

"What? I still don't understand why on earth you think it's necessary I do that."

"Because of what it is doing?" Gary said as if he thought Tam was a few sandwiches short of a picnic.

"But ... I ..." He shook his head again. "What is it doing aside from making Bas and Jules – and me, by the way – happy and stopping their depression from seeping out into the world? What is it doing aside from breaking a cruel curse that was never justified and has caused so much pain and anguish and separated a loving family for thousands of years? What is it doing aside from giving back two magical Beings their Christmas Spirit and helping them to spread their cheer and goodwill?"

"That's what you think it did?" Gary snorted again, his mouth twisting sideways and the look in his eyes said he truly thought Tam a bit simple.

"That's what I know it did," Tam said, crossing his arms and giving Gary a bit of his own 'what the fuck, man!' look back at him.

Gary sighed heavily. "I thought you were far more astute than you obviously are. It seems I gave you too much credit."

"Gary, that's unkind," Merry admonished from inside her globe.

"Maybe it is," he said belligerently. "But well-deserved given what his wish has done."

Tam threw his hands up in the air. "I'm sick of this. You keep talking as if I know what you are talking about, but I don't. So just tell me plain and simple: what do you think the Christmas wish Bas and I made – and Santa granted by the way – has done that is so bad that you want me to unwish it when un-wishing it will send the two people I love back into the kind of pain nobody deserves to endure let alone two good people like they are?"

Gary made a sound of incredulity and waved his hand

between the two globes. "Did you not see what happened when they ended up in the same room together?"

Tam frowned. "Umm, if you're talking about the kissing and dry humping, then yeah, I did see that – wish I could unsee it if truth be told – but I don't see what that has to do with my Christmas wish. It is well known in the pantheons that Santa and Merry have always been a bit on the PDA side of things through all the centuries they've been together."

"He's right," Santa said. "We've always been loving."

Gary screwed his face up, his entire body shaking as if he was enraged, but when he spoke, his voice was even and emotionless. "Yes, you have. And if a bit of PDA was all this was, then I wouldn't be worried. Everyone needs to blow off steam at times, I get that. Believe me, I do. But this is not that. What you two have been doing all over the place in the last few hours since these shenanigans began has been more than any elf can handle. It is by no means healthy or normal."

"It's been fun though," Merry said coquettishly, raising her eyebrows seductively at her husband as she pushed up against the glass.

"Stop that!" Gary said, lifting a finger. "Or I will fill your globe with a snow storm that will cool your jets for you."

Merry jerked back from the glass as she glared at him. "That will be unnecessary."

"Good." He then turned to glare at Tam, pointing back at the globes behind him. "See what you've done!"

Tam shrugged helplessly. "I still fail to see how my wish has caused them to be oversexed all of a sudden."

"Oversexed? Oversexed!" Gary said, obviously incensed. "If that's all it was I'd dump them in a cabin in the middle of nowhere and let them go at it until they'd gotten it out of their system."

"Then why don't you do that if their loving is distressing you so much?"

"Because it is not coming from them, it's coming from your Bas and Jules. From the energy emanating from them."

"That?" Tam snorted and waved his hand – trying for nonchalance even though he was a little surprised their sexual energy had reached as far as the North Pole already. "That should fade away when Bas and Jules' energy stops seeping into the ley-lines."

"You think this is a ley-lines issue?" Gary made an aggravated growl sound as he glowered at Tam. "This is far worse than a ley-lines issue. Energy affected ley-lines would not affect Santa the way this has. No, it's the breaking of the curse in the way it was never meant to be broken that has caused this to happen. It created a link between Bas and Jules and Santa so that their sexual energy is feeding straight into him – and because of the time of year it is, that means it is feeding into everyone else."

"Oh."

"Yes, oh. And unlike ley-lines affected sexual energy, this can't be driven out of their systems by any amount of sexual relief either. In fact, having sex makes it worse. I have barely been able to stop them once they got started. So far I've had to use more and more of my magic to separate them multiple times since your wish was granted and, despite promising to stay apart, they don't seem capable of doing so. Now I've been forced to globe them so their behaviour doesn't keep affecting the world around them."

"Well can't you keep them in the globes until whatever this is passes?"

"You're not listening to me. It's. Not. Going. To. Pass!"

Gary shouted, his face seriously red. "Besides, even if I could do that, I can't do it now. Have you forgotten what time of year it is? Santa Claus is supposed to be in his chair sharing his powers with the world, sending out Christmas Spirit and granting Christmas wishes – non-dangerous to the world Christmas wishes. If I have to keep him in this particular globe, he can't do that."

"Can't you let him out and keep Merry in hers?"

"Hey!" Merry said. "Don't give him ideas!"

Gary shot her a displeased look before turning that displeasure back on Tam who had to stop himself from backing up further across the room – much further and he'd be out the window and in the cold. "I don't need ideas. I've already thought of doing that, but it won't work. The rebound from the wish is too powerful. They will find their way to each other no matter what I do. Besides, while Santa is thinking about having sex every which way with his wife, he's not giving his all to his responsibilities, which will have serious repercussions on not only this world, but all the Realms."

"What? How?"

"Because," Gary said as if explaining to a simpleton. "What is happening is powerful enough to push through time and space and into the Aether. And very soon, all anyone will be doing anywhere is sex. Sex, sex and more sex. All the time. To the detriment of everything else. People will sex themselves to death. You think that Bas and Jules' depression would have had a detrimental effect on the world? Well, it is nothing in comparison to what will happen if we don't stop the rebound effect of your wish."

"Ahh, that sounds bad—"

"You think?"

"But I still don't see what it has to do with my wish.

This could have been caused by something else. Have you thought of that?"

"I thought of that, but quickly dismissed it when I tracked the link back to Jules and Bas. They are the source of the power affecting these two – and Santa and Merry's sexual energy is quickly affecting everything in the North Pole and soon will be affecting everyone everywhere if we don't stop it. Just look out the window if you don't believe me."

Tam turned to look out the window just behind him – and instantly wished he hadn't. A reindeer orgy was going on in the snow and in the sky, backlit by the Northern Lights in a way that made it difficult to unsee what he was seeing. But that wasn't the worst of it. In the snow all around the house, in the windows of the other houses he could see, elves and creatures of all sorts were having riotous, orgiastic sex.

Shuddering, and rubbing his eyes hard to try to rid them of the images he was afraid would never go away, he turned back to Gary. "I really didn't need to see that."

"*You* didn't need to see it! *You didn't need to see it?* Imagine how I felt when I saw my youngest sisters going at it with Lady Sith and Thor who are visiting from Valhalla for the season. All ten of them at once! They were virgins until your bloody wish turned them into Asgardian sex slaves."

Tam blanched – he'd had the misfortune of witnessing a couple of Lady Sith and Thor's orgies when he'd been a younger cupid, and they weren't for the faint of heart. Even so, he said, "I'm sure it's not that bad."

"It *is* that bad. It's worse than that bad because it won't stop with humanoid creatures being with humanoid creatures and animal creatures being with animal creatures.

Very soon all boundaries of what is right and wrong will be broken and the horror of inappropriate inter-species copulation will be the least of our worries. I hope I'm making myself clear because I don't really want to speak the words for fear of making it reality given the magics flying around right now."

Tam raised his hand, feeling a little sick. "No, please, don't speak it. I get what you're inferring. Whatever is happening will lead to all kinds of horrific things if we don't stop it. But I still don't understand why you think this has to do with my wish."

"I told you. I traced it back to its origin."

"Which was my Christmas wish?"

"Yes."

"But how? My Christmas wish was that Jules and Bas would gain back their Christmas Spirit to help them through not only Christmas but the next few months as we seek the final information to break their curse finally on Valentine's Eve."

"Which would have been fine if that's all the wish had done. But it didn't, did it?" Gary raised his brows at Tam as if encouraging him to finish the thought.

Tam's mind ran over everything that had been said, everything that had happened, trying to grasp a hold of whatever it was that Gary wanted him to grasp a hold of. Then suddenly he gasped. "Clodia put something else nasty in the curse."

Gary threw his arms up in the air. "Finally! The penny drops. Yes, that evil bitch-witch put something definitely nasty in the curse to ensure it couldn't be broken by anyone with magic greater than her. The only way to break it was by the laws that affect curses. Either she had to break it, or what she'd done has to be repeated in the same place with the same magical energies on the exact anniversary at the same time as she had cast the curse."

"But why sexual energy. Why would it choose that energy to take from Bas and Jules and not something far more negative?" Tam asked, gesturing outside and then at Santa and Merry who were starting to rub up against the glass in the globes again and shooting each other looks that were better left for private moments. He quickly looked away.

Gary glanced at the globes and let out an aggravated sigh. He waved his hand and suddenly the globes filled with swirling snow.

"Hey!" Santa and Merry shouted together.

"You need to cool down," Gary shouted back. "It also helps that you can't see each other. And that we can't see you." The last was muttered almost under his breath. He shuddered and then turned back to glare at Tam. "Why sexual energy you ask?"

"Umm, yeah."

"Because – and I can't believe I have to point this out to a cupid so I will say it slowly for you," he said. "Sexual. Energy," he said, taking a step forward for every punctuated word. "Is. More. Powerful. And. Destructive. Than. Any. Form. Of. Negative. Energy. If. It's. Allowed. To. Run. Rampant."

Tam had backed up right to the window, but Gary didn't stop until he was standing right in front of him. The elf lifted his hand and poked a hard, poky finger into Tam's chest with every last word. "Do. You. Get. It. Now?"

Unfortunately, Tam finally did.

He glanced at the two globes, swirling with snow, and the two figures who were once again splayed up against the glass in each globe, writhing and making sexual gestures at each other despite the snowstorm going on in the globe around them. Behind him through the glass he could hear the sounds of sexual pleasure rising above the sound of the snow storm that was now raging outside. A snow storm he realised that was being affected by the intense emotions emanating from every living creature in the North Pole.

He looked down at Gary with a horrible sinking feeling growing inside him, threatening to take him down. Because Gary was right – he was going to have to find a way to undo his wish.

THIRTEEN

Bas was exhausted but that didn't stop him from making love with Jules again right in the middle of the lounge room floor. He couldn't believe Jules jumped him like she did before she'd even finished hanging the wreath over the fireplace. She'd looked down at him as he'd stood holding up the wreath while she hung it on the hooks he'd hammered in with his magic. He'd smiled up at her and then she jumped down from the ladder into his arms, her mouth clashing with his, her hands tearing at his t-shirt.

She was wild and insatiable and he couldn't help meeting her wildness and insatiableness with his own. They didn't even stop when the ladder had crashed to the floor, hitting one of Violetta's priceless antique family heirloom pieces of furniture on the way down. He did pause, worried – Violetta was incredibly house proud and would be very upset if a piece of her valuable inherited furnishings was damaged – but Jules said, her words buzzing against his lips, "You can fix it later with your magic," and then attacked that spot on his neck she knew drove him wild, nipping at it before licking the sting better and then wrapping her mouth right over it to suck it.

He'd end up with a love bite, but he truly didn't care. In fact, it gave him ideas about marking her too.

He didn't think anything more about the damage they caused as they rolled around the floor – ignoring the crashing of the Christmas trees they'd already set up and the little stings on his back and side as they crunched over the broken ornaments that fell off the felled trees.

It wasn't until they had finished and he came down from the bliss that was orgasming with Jules that he felt the sting, remembered the crashes, and looked around.

Holy crap! It looked like a tornado had torn through the room.

A part of him didn't want to care. A part of him just wanted to lie there, holding Jules' naked body against his, and contemplate how long it would take him to recover so he could start the madness all over again.

The other part of him was screaming at him that something was horribly wrong.

He didn't want to listen to that voice. It had been screaming at him almost from the very moment he'd realised the curse was broken. He'd thought it was simply the fact it was so difficult to truly believe the curse was finally broken. But it was becoming increasingly difficult to ignore the feeling that something was wrong – terribly wrong. He truly wished he could simply lose himself in the glory of being with Jules like this and having the curse gone, but he couldn't shove his head in the sand and ignore that fact any longer.

Because this was not normal. The destruction they'd wrought on the room was not the normal expression of love

– it was out of character for both him and Jules. Most especially Jules. And not just because of the destruction.

She would never make love in a room that her grandmama – or anyone for that matter – could walk into at any time. She also wouldn't do anything that would cause damage to furnishings in this house or to her Christmas decorations, even if it could be fixed with magic. It would also upset her terribly under any normal circumstance to know that they had been so lost in their own pleasure that they hadn't cared about damaging the house and its belongings. That they hadn't cared about the fact they had torn down some of the decorations they'd put up as they'd rolled around in the wreath that had still been hanging loose, yanking down the part they'd fixed to the wall, pulling plugs of plaster with it and knocking over two of the beautifully decorated Christmas trees they'd spent hours putting up.

It was not like Jules to be so uncaring about any of it. But right now she was lying in his arms, smiling, seemingly uncaring about the fact they were lying in the middle of such damage. Completely naked. Where anyone could walk in and see them.

It wasn't like her. Not like her at all.

And it wasn't like him either. Normally he would have stopped the moment the ladder had fallen and hit the sideboard, chipping its beautiful, polished surface. He would have done more than simply noticed the Christmas trees they'd knocked over and the crunch of ornaments under their feet as they'd stumbled around. He particularly would have cared about - and not just noticed - the destroyed ornaments as they'd rolled across the floor. The discomfort of the small cuts and slices in their skin would normally have stopped him – and Jules – from continuing. Particularly as he would normally have cared about Jules being hurt by them.

But neither of them had cared, the driving *need* over-riding anything else. It wasn't that he hadn't noticed the damage – to the room and to his body – but in the moment with the need driving him to take and feel everything she could make him feel, he quite simply hadn't cared.

But now the sexual urges driving him in the insanity of simply *feeling* were abated somewhat due to the aston-ishing heights of his orgasm, that part of him that did care was getting louder. And louder. And he could no longer ignore it.

Something was wrong with him and Jules. Horribly wrong. And he had to do something about it before that insane need took over again and he was incapable once more of caring or noticing anything but her and what he wanted to feel with her; inside her.

But what was wrong? And what could he do about it?

Maybe first he needed to figure out if Jules sensed the same wrongness he did.

He shifted, his hand slicking over her skin. Hells, they had both worked up a sweat. He looked down at her as he lifted his hand – a hand covered in blood.

He sat up abruptly, unsettling Jules as he pulled her up with him, his gaze roving over her blood-spattered body.

"Bas," she complained.

"Jules. You're bleeding." Of course she was. What did he think would happen when they'd rolled across broken plastic and glass ornaments? It just made him aware there truly was something wrong because the fact she'd been injured too hadn't registered on him even when he'd thought of the possibility only moments ago.

Jules was looking up at him with such confusion.

"What are you talking about? I'm not bleeding. It's not my time of the month."

"No. Not that kind of bleeding. You're bleeding." He held up his hands to show her – they were both covered in blood.

She gasped and grabbed his hands in hers – her hands were also covered in blood. "What the Hells?" She looked down at herself and then at him. "What happened? Why are we covered in blood?"

He tore his gaze away from her and looked once more over the damage around them. Broken ornaments were scattered across the blood-smeared carpet, showing exactly where they'd rolled while busy making love to each other.

Given Jules was now looking around, brow furrowed in obvious confusion, she hadn't even registered that they'd been cut by the ornaments they'd crushed under them as they'd rolled around. "Oh Gods. What did we do?"

He shook his head as his gaze returned to hers. "There is something wrong, Jules. Something wrong with us."

"Yes there is." She sucked in a shuddering breath. "If Violetta comes back and sees this mess, she's going to kill us and then something will truly be wrong with us. We better clean this up. Clean ourselves up. Then we need to start decorating again."

"Decorating? What? Is that all you're worried about?"

She frowned at him. "What else is there to be worried about? We still have so much work to do." She gestured around her. "Even more than we had before we gave into passion and did this." She giggled. "We were a bit naughty."

"A bit naughty?"

She nodded and giggled again – giggled? Jules didn't giggle! "We better make sure next time that we get back to my room and only make love there. I suppose it was my fault though. I did jump your bones this time." She licked her lips and waggled her eyebrows. "Such lovely bones." She bit her lips seductively – Bas' cock twitched in response and it took every bit of control he still had not to lean forward and kiss those lips he had hungered for thousands of years and lose himself once again in the glory of making love to Jules.

Despite the orgasm they'd both just come down from, the urge to take her was rising once more, threatening to overwhelm all sense, all control, like something was inexorably pushing him towards her.

Like it was coming from outside of him and not inside of him.

What the ever loving fuck?!

Jules reached for him, the urge obviously pushing at her too. Centuries ago she had gloried in making love with him, but not like this. Not with this almost forced urgency.

And certainly not with both of them covered in cuts and blood and in the middle of the destruction of a room that Jules – and Violetta – loved and treasured.

"No, Jules, stop," he said, using every ounce of control he still had to clasp her wrists in his hands and holding her at bay. She was trembling, writhing with her need, her face flushed, the scent of her need rising up to meet him, making his mouth water. What the Hells was going on? "This is bad. This is really bad," he said.

She shook her head, eyes almost wild now as she struggled against his hold, trying to push her body closer to his. "Not bad. Nothing between us could ever be bad. Not when it is this good. Not when we've waited this long."

"No, Jules, stop," he said roughly. "Try to fight against the need. It's not normal. Not natural. A part of you has to feel that. Please tell me a part of you feels that."

She blinked rapidly. "I ... I ..." She shook her head, eyes flaring wide as they focused on the blood on his chest. "Bas! What's going on? What's wrong with us?"

"I don't know. But something is wrong. Terribly wrong." He glanced around him at the destruction of the room.

Jules gasped as her gaze followed his and she registered – truly registered – the destruction around them. "Goddess! Did we do this?" She knew they had – deep inside her, she knew, but it was hard to reconcile it with the knowledge that she would never knowingly do something like this.

Bas nodded. "We did. I barely remember it, but we did."

"I-I ... the memory of it is barely a whisper in my mind. And it's being pushed back again. I am struggling to hold onto it."

"Hold onto it. Hold on," Bas said, voice as strained as hers was. "We can't give in to the need to lose ourselves in each other again until we know what's going on."

Jules nodded jerkily, tears blurring her vision. She couldn't believe she'd been a party to wrecking her grand-mama's precious lounge room like this – a room she loved; a room that held so many precious memories. She also couldn't believe she'd been party to ruining the decorations she and Bas had spent so much time lovingly putting up. She wouldn't do this. Couldn't do this. And yet ...

She had. They had. They'd been lost in carnal need – she couldn't even claim they were making love because she had been driven by pure lust – and hadn't cared about the damage they'd done to the room or each other. The knowledge of it – the shock of it – was the only thing that was helping her to hold the rampaging lust at bay even though her entire body was burning with the need to take Bas inside her once again and ride him until the world exploded around them once more.

She shuddered as she fought back that need, gritted her teeth so hard her jaw hurt. But that was okay because that hurt was helping her to stay in her right mind in this moment along with her horror over what she'd been party to doing. But she was aware it was a thin thread she was grasping – the insanity she'd lost herself to over and over again ever since the curse had been broken was a rampaging beast inside her that she was afraid would prove stronger than her will and her sense of right.

Desperately, her gaze sought out Bas'. He nodded as if he could read her mind. "I know. I feel it too. But we have to fight it until we know what is causing it."

She nodded jerkily again and sucked in a shaky breath. "I can do it."

"I know you can," he said, letting her go.

They stood gingerly trying not to touch each other. When they were standing he edged away from her, a pained expression on his face.

Goddess! She hated that he was in pain. She wanted to stop him from ever being in pain. She—

She caught herself just before she surged towards him without thought. Stumbling back from him, she tripped over the angel she'd not so long ago proudly set on top of the Christmas tree that had been in the corner nearest to the fireplace but was now sprawled over the floor, precious decorations scattered and broken around it.

"Jules!" Bas said, reaching for her as she fell.

"No! Don't!" she cried, even as she hit the floor hard, the breath punching out of her, a broken shard of some-thing slicing into her leg.

"Jules – your leg!" Bas moved towards her again.

She held her hands up. "No. Don't touch me. You can't touch me."

He hesitated a few feet away, his expression showing just how torn he was ... how distressed he was. "I know. But you're hurt."

"I'll be fine. It's just a little cut." She looked down at the fresh cut to her leg as she stood, limping sideways to find a clear piece of floor. It was bleeding but it wasn't bad. She let her gaze rove around the room again. "We have to fix this before Grandmama comes back with the lights she went out to buy."

"We do." Her eyes returned to him just in time to see his gaze skirting down her body and then back up to her face. "But we need to take care of your injuries first."

She gasped again, but not because she had suddenly become aware of the stings of all the cuts on her body that she'd not noticed when they'd happened. It was because she suddenly became aware of the fact she was covered in sticky, drying blood – hers and Bastien's. While she had been aware he too was covered in blood, the fact hadn't really sunk in until right now. "You're hurt too. We need to take care of your injuries too," she said, her gaze roving over his naked, blood-covered body, trying to stop herself from going over to him to properly check him out.

"My demi-Godly powers will heal my cuts in the next half an hour or so – although I will need to shower to remove all this blood. But you don't have your powers back, so will need yours tended to." He took a step towards her. "I should use my healing magic to take care of it for you."

She shook her head and took a cautious step back. "No. I don't think we can trust ourselves to be that close right now. I will go and get the first aid kit and disinfect the cuts and bandage up the worst ones after I've had a shower."

"What about the ones on your back that you can't reach?"

She bit her lip, the little press of pain helping her to stay in control – his worry over her was soooo sexy she wanted to—

She shook her head. Holy crap! What was wrong with her? They were both injured and covered in blood and were standing naked in something close to a disaster zone. How could she have been thinking of having sex with him again?

She took another step back. "I will manage. And if I can't, I'll ask Grandmama to help me when she gets back." She wasn't sure how she was going to explain the injuries – although if they didn't get this mess cleaned up before Violetta got back, then that was the least of the explaining she'd have to do. "We really need to clean this up."

Bas took a step away from her, tearing his gaze from hers to look around the room. "I will take care of it. You go and have a shower and tend to your wounds."

"Are you sure?"

He nodded, still not looking at her, his chest moving up and down fast and hard as if he'd just run a marathon. "I think it will be best. I'm struggling not to go to you right now and—"

She held her hand up. "I know. But don't say it. Speaking the need out loud will just make it worse."

"You're right. So go. I think it will be best if we stay apart for now."

She sucked in a shaky breath. "I think you're right." She scooped up her clothing that was scattered over the floor – most of it was ripped. When she straightened she blanched and pointed towards the door. "Bas, you need to move. You're blocking the way out."

"Oh, right." He began to edge sideways, his movements

stiff and jerky as if he was fighting himself. And he probably was. But still he was managing to move and was using his magic to make a clear path for her through the detritus of broken ornaments, Christmas trees and furnishings they'd somehow managed to topple and damage while they'd—

She shook her head. No. She couldn't even let herself think about what they'd done to make the room look like this.

"Jules, you better go now," Bas said tightly. He was standing in front of the window furthest away from the doorway she needed to exit out of.

"Yes." It was so hard to move though. But she forced one foot forward, then the other, her muscles trembling with the effort. She wanted to run from the room and away from what she'd done here, but the insane urges driving her wouldn't let her, so she had to be content with slowly making her way to the door, forcing herself one step at a time from the room she'd destroyed with her lover and across the foyer to the sweeping staircase that led to the upstairs left wing of Steven's House where her bedroom and en-suite lay.

She was sweating and trembling by the time she made it into her bathroom, her skin slick with the sweat of exertion as much as it was sticky with drying blood. Everything hurt. But that was fine because it was helping her to hold onto her control. And she had to hold onto her control. Because it would be too easy to let go and race back downstairs to where Bas was even now cleaning up their mess – she could feel the pulse of his magic as an echo in the air – and throw herself at him once again.

She couldn't believe she'd been so voracious. Couldn't believe she had it in her to be like that. She'd always wondered if she was indeed frigid in some way because she'd never been able to let herself go with anyone in that way.

Although, come to think of it, that was probably the curse working its nasty tendrils through her.

The curse!

The thought hit her as she turned on the shower and stepped under the spray, shivering as the cold water sluiced over her – she couldn't allow herself the comfort of a warm shower. She stared at her feet, watching the blood-tinged water swirl on the tiled floor and down the drain. They'd thought Bas' wish had washed the curse away much the same as this water was doing to the blood on her body. But had it truly gotten rid of the curse? Or was it somehow still holding onto them with one of the tendrils that had worked its way into them over the centuries as it had deepened its hold? Was it the curse that was causing this insanity of desire and lust to overtake them to the exclusion of all else?

It was something she needed to find out. Because if it was, then they needed to do something about it.

Even if it meant finding a way to put the curse back in place.

Because this kind of desire wasn't normal. It wasn't good. In fact, it could damage more than just the lounge room and the Christmas decorations she loved so dearly. It was why love potions were some of the most dangerous magic a witch could wield because they were driven by unhealthy desire and lust and not true, deep, giving love.

And if that's what the curse had made her and Bas fall into, no matter that they did truly love each other in all the right ways, they had to find a way to stop it.

Because unthinking lust like this could destroy the world.

FOURTEEN

"Oh, I thought you'd be further along than this."

Bas turned to see Violetta standing at the lounge room door, a bag from Jules' favourite Christmas decorations store in her hand.

"I have the extra lights she wanted." She frowned. "Why did you move that Christmas tree over a few inches? I thought it was perfect where it was."

Bas tried not to roll his eyes at himself – of course Violetta would remember exactly where everything was in her beautifully appointed house – even the Christmas decorations she let Jules put up every year. He should have taken more notice of where she and Jules had placed everything. But then again, he didn't think he'd be cleaning up after his love and he had destroyed the room with a lustful romp of inappropriate sex. Normally there would have been no reason for him to remember the placement of anything, but this was far from normal.

He turned back to the decoration he'd been in the middle of hanging, waved his hand and let his magic finish the job – so thankful that he'd finished cleaning everything up twenty minutes ago, including himself and had put cotton pants and a t-shirt on – one Jules had given him two years ago with a crazy goat on the front in a Santa hat that said, 'Seasons Bleatings!'

Once the wreath was set in place, he waved his hand and moved the Christmas tree over a few centimetres. "Better?" he asked, turning back to face Violetta.

"Yes." Her lips twitched into a smile and she pointed at his t-shirt. "I see you gave in to the Christmas cheer as well."

He raised his brows and she gestured at the necklace and earrings she sported – red, green and gold bells hung beside leaping reindeer. They weren't anything close to the tasteful pieces in gold and silver she usually wore. She touched them as she said, "I was so happy to see her happy once more that I put on this ghastly jewellery she wanted me to wear last year."

"You wore them out?"

She shrugged. "I couldn't bring myself to take them off even when I was going out in public. It seemed like a betrayal of her Christmas Spirit." She fiddled with the necklace as she looked around the room. "Where is Jules by the way? I thought she'd be in here finishing this room with you before moving on to the other rooms down here."

Noticing a little drop of blood on the carpet under the lounge, he flicked it away with a drop of cleaning magic before Violetta could see it and, trying to keep his face from showing his level of worry – and the urge to go upstairs and give into the madness once more – said, "She's upstairs I think."

Violetta frowned. "You think? I thought you'd be keeping close tabs on her now the curse has been broken." Her eyes flared as she took a step forward. "Don't tell me she had a reaction to the magic we've been using to put up the decorations. I would never have agreed to putting all those decorations up in the foyer or outside if I thought she was still having allergy issues."

Bas held his hands up. "No. No. It's not that at all. She's not reacting badly to the magic we've both used."

"Oh," Violetta said, hand clutching at her chest. "That's such a relief." She let out a loud breath, her fringe fluttering a little. "I keep waiting for the other shoe to drop and I—" Her eyes narrowed as she looked at him and her head tipped to the side a little. "It has dropped, hasn't it? You said she's not reacting to the magic but she is reacting to something, isn't she? As you are if I'm reading your expression correctly. You look like you're in pain."

Bas grimaced – Violetta had always been highly intelligent and had a finely tuned radar for picking up what was said between the lines, as well as reading people incredibly well. He should have known she'd pick up something was wrong almost as soon as she entered the house.

"What?" she asked, taking a hesitant step towards him. "What's happened?"

"Nothing." She looked daggers at him – her expression clearly saying, 'bullshit someone who enjoys the taste of it'. He raised his hands again. "Nothing that couldn't be fixed with a little magic ... and a huge amount of self-control."

"Ah, so that explains the tree," she said, mouth screwing to the side. "So what happened?"

"A little bit of unexpected destruction when Jules ... um ... well she ... we ..." Gods this was more difficult than he'd expected. He was a cupid for Gods' sake! He shouldn't be embarrassed about having had sex. And yet, telling Violetta what had happened in this room was suddenly one of the hardest things he'd ever done.

She put her hands on her hips, tapping her forefingers against the silk of her violet skirt. "Come on. Spit it out. What did you both do?"

He looked away from her. "We had sex. Here. In this room."

"I gathered that when you said 'here'. So, you went a little overboard?"

He grimaced again. "More than a little. She was on the ladder and looked down at me and then suddenly she was on top of me and we were naked and rolling around and ..." He shook his head, the heat of the memory flushing through him, making it even more difficult not to just open a portal and flash himself up to Jules where she was probably still locked in her bedroom to stop herself from running down here to him. "You don't need the details—"

"No, I most certainly don't," Violetta said dryly as she finally entered the room and made her way to the lounge. "But I gather you both lost yourself and made a mess."

Bas nodded. "A big one. We didn't even notice that we'd damaged things, knocked the trees down and had rolled over the decorations."

"Didn't they break?"

"Yes they did."

"Didn't they cut you then?"

"Yes, they did."

"And that didn't stop you?"

"Not even a little bit. It wasn't until after when I saw the blood on Jules and then myself that I realised how bad it had been."

"You healed though I see, so it couldn't have been that bad." Violetta sat on the elegant cream lounge, the bag at her feet. "I haven't been gone long and see you are all healed up. I expect you healed Jules too – so as long as you cleaned up, I'm not going to take either of you to task other than to say maybe keep the sexual gymnastics to the private areas of the house – namely your bedrooms."

He hissed out a breath between his teeth. "I haven't healed Jules."

"What?" Violetta jumped to her feet. "Why?"

"I couldn't go near her. It was all we could do to hold ourselves back and not start the madness all over again."

"Madness?"

He nodded. "That's what it felt like ... what it still feels like."

"You're still fighting it now?"

He gritted his teeth and said through them, "Yes."

"It's that bad?"

"Yes."

"For both of you?"

"Yes."

Violetta frowned and tapped her chin with her forefinger. "Well, this isn't good."

"You reckon?"

She snapped a look at him and he made a 'sorry' face. She waved him off before he could manage to open his mouth though. "I thought I felt something a little strange as I drove into the neighbourhood. And there was some serious PDA going on between Mr and Mrs Simonson in their front yard a few doors up, but I dismissed it given I know they have been going to a lot of parties and thought maybe they'd just returned from one and had over imbibed. But maybe that wasn't what it was at all."

"Shit. It's affecting other people?"

She shrugged. "Maybe. I'll have to look into it."

"You're not feeling it, are you?"

She shifted a little. "I'm feeling something, although

nothing close to what you said you both experienced. I do have my personal shields up though – habit from so many years of shielding Jules from my magic – so I am unlikely to be affected by any wayward emotions coming from you and Jules quite yet." She sighed and looked around then back at him. "I think I better go and check on Jules then. See if she needs help with her injuries."

"She will need help with some of the cuts on her back."

She pressed her lips together. "No doubt." She sighed deeply. "Very well. I'll go and take care of Jules while you stay down here and ..." She gestured at the bag of lights and the boxes of decorations still piled out in the foyer. "You finish in here and then get a start on the dining room and kitchen. I imagine you need to keep yourself busy."

"I certainly do. Putting all this up is the only thing stop-ping me from charging up the stairs and bashing Jules' door down right now."

Violetta cleared her throat. "Well, we can't have that. Do you need me to put a shield spell up around you or Jules?"

He shook his head sadly. "I'm not sure it will help. I'm afraid I will find some way to bash it down if I lose control."

"A sleep spell then?"

"Maybe. If either of us makes a move towards the other, it might be the only thing that can stop us. But for now, I think doing this is helping enough. And given Jules is still upstairs, she's found some way of holding onto her control enough to stop herself from coming down here and jumping me again."

"Well, okay." She cleared her throat again. "Not the conversation I thought I'd be having today."

"Sorry."

"Not your fault." She gave him a half smile and waved

her hand. "I'm not sure whose fault this is, but we will get to the bottom of it as soon as I have made certain Jules is okay."

"You'll be heading to the library?"

"Research into sex spells seems our best bet for now."

"Should I go down there right now and start?"

She shook her head. "No. Jules will be of more use to me in the research department to begin with and given you can't be in the same room together, I think it's best you keep yourself busy finishing the decorating while I help Jules with her wounds and then accompany her down to the library."

"Let me know before you cross the foyer. I think it's best I'm as far away from her as I can be when you come down – so I should be in the kitchen when you go to the library."

"I will buzz the old intercom then to let you know."

"Sounds good."

She made her way to the door but before she exited it, she turned back to him. "She will be upset that she can't help you to put the decorations up like usual, so just make sure they are done in the way that will please her the most. I know you know how that should be."

"I do. I will."

"Good. Because after we get to the bottom of what is causing this ... sexual overexertion ... in you two, she'll want to celebrate her first Christmas without the curse with as much Christmas Spirit and *joie de Noelle* as possible. And she won't be able to do that if the house isn't appropriately decorated."

"I know that. And I won't stop until it's exactly like she would do it."

"Good. Great." She clapped her hands. "We have a plan, so let's hop to it." She turned and exited the room leaving him standing there staring at the bags of lights she'd left. Jules hadn't told him what she wanted to do with the extra lights, but he had an idea, so he would finish putting up what she'd planned to have in this room – and double check for any more blood spots he'd missed – and then he'd move to the kitchen which is where she always went to town given it was her favourite room in the house.

It helped – it did – to have something to do. But by the Gods he wanted to scratch at the itch that had been growing under his skin ever since Jules had left the room. He resisted it though with gritted teeth and turned back to the decorating, wishing it helped more than it was doing, because if this kept up, he had the choice of going insane or giving in.

And he couldn't give in to whatever this was. He just couldn't. Jules and he deserved so much more after all these years of waiting – and pining on his behalf. They deserved everything lovers could have and so much more.

But not this.

Most definitely not this. Because this ... it was insane and not something he wanted for him and his mate. And he was certain she didn't want it either. Jules deserved to be loved and treasured and be able to love and treasure in equal measure. And when they'd figured this out, that was exactly what he was going to ensure she got.

The thought of the life he would have with Jules helped lift the heavy cloud he'd been under ever since it had become clear something had gone wrong with his wish. It reminded him that he couldn't let the depression slip in again. After so many thousands of years of waiting and pining and feeling so alone sometimes he thought it would break him, he couldn't give up now. Not when he'd had a taste of what life could be like when they were fully clear of the curse and whatever this was.

It did help a little that he could lean into Jules' love of Christmas. The twinkle of the lights around him and the sparkle of the colourful decorations were certainly cheering. This was not part of his pantheon's beliefs, but he had always thrown himself into it, loving to indulge with Jules on her love of this time of year. He loved the joy she took from it.

But it wasn't simply that, he now realised. There was something so much more important behind putting up all this stuff, hearing the carols and Christmas songs and the fun she had buying gifts for them all and then wrapping them up and putting them under the tree. It brought more than a temporary joy in the pretties; it created hope and something to look forward to during the year.

It helped Jules to reconnect with the kindness and happiness that were essential to her soul and enabled her to hold onto those things even when life wasn't so kind. There was far more to her Christmas Spirit than just what she experienced in the five or six weeks around Christmas. It even infected him and Violetta and the members of the Stevens' extended family who came around to help her in her celebration and charity efforts on the day – even though they didn't celebrate themselves, but had their own witch-centric Yule celebrations.

Laughter and happy chatting increased across the day; memories of those who had passed were shared and delighted in; those who arrived in the morning uptight because of work and/or family pressures, were soon relieved of that heaviness and left looking a lot lighter at the end of the day of being in a house filled with happiness and celebration – not just celebration of Christmas, but celebration of family, of life, of love, of friendship, of kindness, of giving and of course charity.

Because that was always a part of Jules' Christmas Spirit – giving to those in need. She bought gifts for underprivileged kids and their parents and put on a big banquet for the homeless and others in need of company and a good feed. She roped the family in to helping serve and look after these people in the afternoon and early evening. And it didn't end on Christmas Day. It just started then. Her charity continued for the rest of the week with her organizing a clothing, toiletries and toy drive to deliver to the major charities that looked after the homeless and at risk women and kids. She roped the entire neighbourhood into the event and they always had truckloads of donations to deliver by New Years Day.

Her charity didn't just last for the Christmas period though. The spirit of charity continued through the entire year with her volunteering at soup kitchens and meals on wheels, visiting the elderly and working with a local charity that organised backpacks with school essentials for underprivileged kids, including vouchers to cover the cost of school uniforms and camps as well as things like school organised swimming lessons – things that many people took for granted but that could mean the world to those who would otherwise miss out.

He hadn't realised before this moment how much she got out of the Christmas period and how it fed her spirit and enabled her to give of herself in these ways. This year, before his Christmas wish, she had been devoid of even the whisper of what Christmas usually gave her. She had been so depressed she hadn't even thought to organise the charity drive, had given up her shifts with meals on wheels and at the soup kitchens and had pulled out of visiting the elderly neighbours she spent time with every week. And there had been no talk of any of the other charity work she was always busy with outside her work in the Stevens' library. She'd even given up working in the library and her joy in books and learning new things had completely disappeared.

He couldn't let this happen to her ever again. He had to make sure she got what she needed out of this Christmas – and every Christmas hereafter – so that she would be the Jules she was always meant to be even if she never got back the magic that should be a part of her.

Even if they never got to be together, he had to ensure her Christmas Spirit never faded because it was amazing how much she brought to the world when that spirit was invested fully within her. He could never let that fade away in her again.

The fucking curse had taken so much more from her than their love. He wouldn't let it take anything more. He would make this the best Christmas she'd ever had. He wasn't certain how given what was going on between them, but he would find a way if it was the last thing he did for her. He would give his life to make sure she lived her life in happiness, empathy and giving. He would—

A portal sparked to life in front of him, the whirling green, gold and red maelstrom of it making the room glow with pulsing light, the wind of its sudden appearance – and its intense strength – making the decorations on the Christmas trees and on the walls jingle, chime and rustle in the shifting air.

"What the Hells?" He stumbled back, almost losing his balance as he tripped over the bag of lights Violetta had left there. Catching himself on the arm of the couch before he ended up on his arse, he struck a defensive pose, ready to face whatever came through the shimmering circle of magic. The only Being who ever came into this house via portal was Tamuel, but his portals were usually blue and purple in colour, so this couldn't be him.

He had no idea who would be powerful enough to break through the wards Violetta set up against such intrusions – Tam was a demi-God and was able to slip through the wards using the peculiar loophole that was essential to the cupid powers that once had been Bas' too. That loophole allowed all cupids to get into any place in the world in the pursuit of their duties. Which was how the younger cupid was able to portal in and out of Stevens House without alerting Violetta through her wards.

He expected to hear Violetta come running down the stairs at any moment to see who was breaking into her house, because surely the wards would be ringing all of the alarms due to this intrusion. But outside of the whooshing sound of the portal, he heard nothing.

Maybe he'd have to fight whoever was breaking into the house all by himself. He wasn't back to full magical strength yet, but he had good command of much of his powers as they slowly returned to him now the curse was broken. He could put up a decent fight and hopefully give Jules and Violetta a chance to properly shield and escape whatever was coming through. He—

All thoughts escaped him as a reindeer with a pulsing red nose leapt through the portal, skidding to a halt on the carpet in front of him. But it wasn't just the reindeer – Rudolph if he wasn't mistaken – that made all thought escape him.

Tam sat on Rudolph's back – eyes closed and looking like he was about to puke – behind an elf with a seriously disapproving expression on his face as he shouted something. Slowly the words came through to Bas' shocked brain ...

"... said not so fast you bloody quadruped. I do not want this bloody cupid to lose his lunch all down the back of my best elf suit!"

Rudolph tossed his head, his nose pulsing even faster, looking a bit like a flashing emergency light.

The elf sucked in a breath as he threw one leg over his mount's neck and dropped to the floor to march around to face the most famous reindeer in the world. "Not your problem! I'll make it your problem you red-nosed horny beast!" He shook his finger in Rudolph's face. "How would you like me to put you in charge of washing the elf clothes once we get back?" Rudolph looked down and shook his head. "I thought not." The elf blew out a breath. "Get down from there Tam before you fall off. Now where is he? I thought Blitzen was following right behind."

Rudolph looked back at him as he walked towards the portal and blew a raspberry.

Neither the elf nor Bas had time to react to any of that because just then another reindeer flew through the portal – a much larger and more muscular reindeer with an impressive ten-point rack – with a very large, red- and-white-attired, snowy bearded man on the back of him, yahooing with joy, his arm raised like a bull rider as they came to a skidding halt on the carpet, just stopping a hair's-breadth from Bas.

"Ho-ho-ho, whoa, Blitzen," Santa – it was obviously Santa – said as he dismounted. He unhooked a big, red sack from the reindeer's back, slung it over his shoulder and gave Blitzen a whacking pat on the whither. "Thank you for that exciting ride, my friend. You can head back and let Mrs Claus know we got here safely. I'll send a message through when we're done here and you can come back and fetch me."

Blitzen nodded his head, turned and jumped back through the portal.

"Ahh, he's a good lad," Santa said as the huge reindeer disappeared. Then, smiling broadly, he strode forward, shoving his hand out towards Bas. "Well met, young cupid!"

Unable to think past the fact Santa obviously wanted to shake his hand, Bas put his hand out. Their palms met and the large – not round-tummy large, but muscled and huge-shouldered and six foot six large – man gave a hearty shake that almost made Bas stumble forward with the enthusiasm of it. But the action was enough to shake Bas out of his shocked stupor.

He managed to disengage from Santa and then turned to Tam who had dismounted shakily. "What the ever loving Hells is going on, Tam?"

CHAPTER

FIFTEEN

"That's exactly what I'm here to discuss with you." Tam wiped a hand across his brow and sidled away from the reindeer who had turned to stare at him.

Clearly in his head Tam heard, *"What? Aren't you going to thank me? That must have been the most exciting ride in your life. Enjoyable no?"*

"No, I didn't enjoy the ride," he snapped, eyes narrowing at the crazy reindeer. "I think you purposefully made that ride even worse than the first."

Rudolph was looking at him, eyes swirling wildly in a way that made Tam want to puke. He took in a deep breath and forced himself not to look at the crazily swirling eyes. "And no, I'm not going to thank you for putting some excitement in my life. My life is quite exciting enough."

The reindeer sniggered and strode away to nibble at one of the house plants in the corner. The portal snapped closed with a whoomph as he did.

"Umm, can you please not do that," Bas asked,

sounding more unsure than Tam had ever heard him sound – no wonder given it was not obvious how the most famous reindeer in the world would react. "Violetta – the witch who owns this house – is rather particular about her plants. She'd be very upset if you ate any of them."

"Ho-ho-ho," Santa chuffed. "Portalling always makes my bright-nosed friend exceptionally hungry." He put the sack on the ground and tucked his thumbs in his black belt and looked indulgently at his lead reindeer.

"I can get him some carrots to eat," Bas suggested, gaze flicking between the man in the big red and white coat and the nose-glowing reindeer munching at the greenery. "And some water if you're thirsty?"

"He'd prefer a stiff Scotch and a plate of fruit cake or mince tarts if you've got them," Gary said matter-of-factly.

"I thought he preferred spiced rum," Tam said.

"With his chai latte, yes, but to drink neat, he prefers a good Single Malt."

"Too right," Santa said jovially. "And if you don't want him to eat all the plants in the room in the next ten minutes, you better get him that drink sooner rather than later. For myself, I could do with a nice cup of Earl Grey."

Bas stared at the room around him as if worried that if he left, more than the plants might be damaged.

"Why don't we go with you," Tam suggested. "To the kitchen. All of us," he said pointedly towards Rudolph.

"Wonderful idea," Santa said, unhooking his thumbs from his belt to clap his hands together – making an altogether thunderous sound that made everyone in the room flinch. "I'm a bit hungry myself, truth be told."

"Ah, okay, then come this way," Bas said, gesturing out the door.

"Come Gary, come Rudolph, come Tamuel. Let's follow our host to the kitchen."

Bas stood there for a moment looking a bit dumbstruck.

"After you," Santa bellowed, picking the sack up and slinging it over his shoulder again.

Bas jumped, blinked, then nodded. "Ah, right. The kitchen." He swiped a bottle of Violetta's best Scotch off a side table near the door and then turned on his heel and exited the room.

Rudolph, seeing the Scotch vanish, clip-clopped after him, Santa and Gary following in his wake. Tam shook his head and followed too – after all, where was he going to go?

Tam wished *he* had somewhere else to go, but that wasn't about to happen. And not because Gary had somehow portal-locked his magic before they had come here on that crazy reindeer's back. He'd said he wasn't taking the chance that Tam would try to run away from the responsibility in front of him.

And while he didn't want to do what they wanted him to do, he had no choice. He had seen the upshot of what his and Bas' wish had done and it was not something that could be allowed to continue. But honestly, why did he have to be the one to ruin his parents' happiness? Why did he have to be the one responsible for putting the curse back in place? It was the last thing he wanted to do.

But it was the only thing he *could* do.

Because if he didn't, if Gary was right, it could destroy the universe. With sex.

Well, not with sex per se. But the upshot of the rebounding curse was that all Beings would soon be unable to do anything other than have riotous sex to the detriment of everything else. Sex that would put an energy out there that was wild and uninhibited and ultimately destructive.

Because while some wildness and a lack of inhibitions was good on occasion, too much would lead to utter chaos – the kind of chaos that would break the bonds between space and time, folding different realities in on themselves and ...

Well, he didn't really want to think about what would happen then. It would be worse than the worse thing anyone could imagine happening – the opposite of the Big Bang, no pun intended.

The Big Un-bang.

And the Big Un-bang would come only after some very painful things happened that even the torturers in Tartarus would find objectionable. Then everything would cease to exist.

He couldn't be responsible for that.

Bas and Jules would not want to be responsible for that either. They would give up their happiness for much less because his parents, in spite of everything that had happened to them, were really good people.

Which was why, after all this was sorted and he had found a way to break the curse as it was always meant to be broken, he would do everything he could to give them everything they deserved. Which included getting Jules' magic back for her.

It wasn't only that they deserved to be happy in love. They deserved to be together forever. And she deserved to be exactly who the Eternal Well and the Fates meant her to be. A truly freakin' powerful witch with the magic gifted to her at birth by a Goddess. A freakin' powerful witch who could live as long as her demi-God mate if she only had her powers.

"Are you coming, Tamuel?"

Santa's bellow – so loud even though they had disappeared out the door and would be close to the kitchen by now which was down a long hallway at the back of the house – had Tam jumping and running after them.

He really didn't want to let Gary be the one to tell Bas what must be done. That elf had a terrible bedside manner and the least Tam could do was to deliver the news with kindness and empathy.

But he hated this with everything in him. He was a cupid. He was supposed to bring love and happiness and joy into the world. That was his *raison d'être*. And yet, for all his good intentions, telling Bas – and then Jules – what had happened was going to be like torture. Worse than torture. For him and for the two people he cared about more than any others in the world.

Sometimes, life sucked the big one.

"Tamuel! Where have you got to boy?"

Tam jumped again then sighed – how did Merry put up with that bellowing voice? – and ran even faster down the hallway and into the kitchen.

Everyone, bar Bas and Rudolph, was seated at the round kitchen table in the breakfast nook, the light from the floor-to-ceiling windows of the hexagonal high-roofed sun nook shining down on Santa like a spotlight, glowing off the red velvet of the sack that hung on the back of the chair. And like an actor in the spotlight, he was lapping up the attention focused on him as he poured the Scotch in a bowl for Rudolph – who stood behind him, big tongue licking his reindeer lips as he watched what Santa was doing. Bas himself was busy on the other side of the kitchen filling up plates with cake and baked goods.

"Ah, Tamuel, there you are. Thought you had made an escape," he said as he placed the bowl of Scotch on the floor for Rudolph, who immediately began to slurp it up.

"Wouldn't dream of it," he said, forcing a smile and

heading over to help Bas carry the plates of snacks to the table. He put down his load and pulled out a chair, sitting heavily. Bas did the same, taking a seat opposite him.

"The kettle is on," Bas said to Santa.

"Wonderful." Santa busied himself filling a plate for Rudolph and placed it on the floor in front of the reindeer next to the now almost empty bowl of Single Malt Scotch.

As he turned to fill a plate for himself, he seemed to become aware that everyone was watching him. He looked up, brow raised. "What?"

"Are you going to take the lead here," Gary said. "Or do you expect me to do it again?"

"Oh-ho-no!" Santa chortled, then shoved a large wedge of fruit cake into his mouth, chewing twice and swallowing it down faster than Tam had seen anyone swallow anything down before. It was rather like watching a boa constrictor swallowing a very large rat.

Tam shuddered at that imagery and tried to refocus on the conversation as Santa said, "You are in fine fettle, Gary."

Gary crossed his arms and pouted. "Do you think I choose to be here? If not for you and your too empathetic heart, I would be back in the North Pole taking care of business there. But no. Here I am in a witch's house, cleaning up your mess once again. I swear, I should demand a raise."

"I don't pay you."

"Well ... I ..." Gary blustered. "Perhaps I should demand you *should* pay me."

"And have your poor mother and father roll over in their graves? Besides, you yourself have told me that elves don't get paid filthy lucre for the work they do in the service of magical good. In fact, when I raised worries about it being a kind of slavery, you were the one who lectured me on the fact that it wasn't slavery because working for magical good is essential to an elf's make-up because they get to feed on the energy created by it – which is payment in a way. To pay you in any normal way would change the dynamics of that and the energy you need to live would dissipate and you would all eventually die. In fact you have lectured me on this more times than I can recount."

Gary stared down at the table, face like a storm cloud and grumbled under his breath. Tam missed most of it but managed to catch something that sounded like, "...don't have to quote my own words back at me."

Silence fell again as Santa – and Rudolph – munched on cake and Gary pouted. Just then, the kettle began to whistle and Bas jumped up to get Santa his tea.

He didn't ask anyone else if they wanted some, but when he returned, he placed four mugs on the table with the teapot, milk and sugar.

"It needs to brew for a moment," he said, sitting down and looking around at the others at the table. After a long moment of silence, he asked, "Is anyone going to tell me why Santa, Rudolph and some elf—"

"Gary. My name's Gary," Gary said, his gaze snapping to Bas. "And I'm not just some elf. I'm Santa Claus' Chief Elf and Major Domo."

"Well, okay ... Gary." Bas glanced around at all of them again. "Is anyone going to tell me why you all portalled into my house and are now sitting in my kitchen eating cake and drinking tea and Violetta's best Scotch." He stared at Rudolph as the reindeer slurped up the last of his Scotch and let out a massive burp.

Bas' eyes flared wide and he pointed at the reindeer. "Did he just tell me this isn't my house?"

Gary stopped pouting long enough to say, "You're a cupid who lives in a witch's house and just recently spent thousands of years as a cat between sunrise and sunset and you're surprised a reindeer can mind-speak?"

"I ... Well, I suppose that's fair," Bas said huskily. "And this might not be my house by law, but I've lived here ever since it was built and will continue to live here for as long as the Stevens allow me to. It is my home. And therefore, it is as much my house as it is anyone else who lives here."

"Touchy touchy," Gary said. "Rudolph, it is the cupid's home." He tipped his head as if listening. "I know, I know. Just eat your cake and stop causing trouble. There's enough of that as it is without you causing more."

Rudolph tipped his head from one side to the other then returned to his plate of fruit cake and mince tarts.

Silence again – just the sound of Santa and Rudolph chewing.

Bas looked between Santa, Rudolph, Gary. Santa raised his brows back at him. "Shall I be mother?" he said, reaching for the teapot.

"Whatever you like," Bas said a little snippily.

Santa didn't take offence. He chortled and went about pouring tea, asking who wanted milk and sugar. Once he was done pouring, he took a sip of his own tea and sat back in his chair with a sigh. "Lovely," he said before shovelling more fruit cake into his mouth.

Nobody else reached for their teas, they simply stared at each other.

When the silence had stretched to extremes and it was obvious neither Santa nor Gary – who'd begun to sip at his tea in a way that said he was doing it so he didn't have to speak - Bas turned to Tam. "So, are you going to tell me what the Hells is going on? Why are you all here?"

"Umm ..." Tam didn't know how to tell him what they'd come here to say.

"Has this got something to do with our wish?"

Tam's brows rose. "Why do you say that?"

"Well ..." Bas's cheeks pinked a little and his gaze dropped away. "Things have become a bit ... weird ... since you left after our wish came true."

Gary sat forward suddenly. "Like sex weird."

Bas' gaze flicked to him. "How did you know that?"

Gary sat back, waving his hand at Santa. "Because your problem has become a universal problem."

Bas frowned. "What the Hells do you mean by that?"

Gary leaned forward and said slowly, each word enunciated as if he spoke to a child who lacked the ability to understand more than the simplest language. "Your. Wish. Has. Turned. Santa. Into. A sex. Starved. Automaton."

"What?"

"It's not that bad," Santa said around a mouthful of cake.

Gary opened his mouth, but Tam held his hand up and said, "Let me tell him."

Gary waved his hand. "I wish you would."

Tam sighed and stared at the table for a moment before looking up at his father. "It seems our wish didn't exactly simply break the curse. It ... created a link between you both and Santa and his missus. The upshot of which is that Santa here, and his wife Merry, are unable to stop from indulging in ... marital congress. Constantly. And because of the time of the year and the fact Santa's energy is focused on going out into the world, it means that slowly but surely, everyone is starting to do the same. To the detriment of everything else."

Bas stared at him for a long moment before he said, "Well, Hells. I knew there was the possibility that our emotional state had broken out of the bounds of the house, but I didn't think you were going to say that."

"Yeah, well ..." Tam reached for a slice of cake and picked it up to put on his plate even though he wasn't hungry. Picking at the cake on the plate in front of him, he forced himself to continue. "It's pretty bad. And ... the only thing that can be done to stop it is—"

"Is to reverse our wish?"

His gaze snapped up to Bas. He nodded jerkily. "Yes." It didn't make it any easier that Bas had said the words he dreaded saying. He looked down at his hands and the destroyed piece of cake on his plate. "I'm so sorry. I never imagined this would happen when I suggested the wish. I thought it would help Jules. Help you. Help everyone. Instead, it made it all worse. It's all my fault and yet, you both are going to be the ones to pay the price for my mistake. I am—"

"Stop."

He turned around to see Jules standing at the doorway. She gripped the doorframe with one hand, knuckles white, as if that grip was the only thing keeping her standing.

"Jules!" Bas said, shoving his chair back with a loud squeal as he stood and began to move towards her. "Where's Violetta?"

"Taking an emergency call from the European Witch Council. We were heading down to the library and I said I would continue down there while she went into the loungeroom to take the call in private. But then I felt ..." She grimaced as she clung to the doorframe. "I knew I had to come here."

Bas lurched forward. "Jules I—"

"No! Don't take another step," she said, her gaze wild,

her face flushed. "It's all I can do not to come over there and jump your bones in front of everyone."

Tam heard in his head clearly, *"I wouldn't mind seeing that."*

He wasn't surprised when Gary said, "Shut up, you pervert," to the reindeer.

He normally would have laughed, but this wasn't a laughing matter. Jules was obviously trying desperately not to race across the room and strip all the clothes from her mates' body – it was most definitely something he didn't want to see. And she was obviously distressed over what she had just heard.

How much had she heard?

Her gaze flickered to him. "I heard enough," she said through gritted teeth. "And even though I don't know you, I know it's not your fault, so stop blaming yourself."

"I—" He shook his head. She was wrong but he wasn't going to argue with her about it now. "You should go upstairs. Stay away from Bas."

She shook her head slowly. "No. If the wish has to be reversed, if I'm going to be cursed again and lose all I've had this last day, then I want to be here when it happens. I want to look at my love and remember for as long as I can that he is my love." She grimaced, turning a little to hold onto the doorframe with both hands. "But I'd appreciate it if one of you could help me to control myself. I seem to have lost the ability."

"You seem to be holding yourself there okay," Gary said.

She shook her head jerkily. "It's taking everything ... I can't hold on much longer."

Her gaze raked across the room to Bas. Tam followed her gaze and saw that Bas too looked like he was being tortured. His entire body was shaking as he leant over the table, hands flat on its surface as if he was trying to dig them into the wood. And the look on his face ... it was horrible to witness. So much pain as he stopped himself from racing across the room to his mate and doing to her what she wanted to do to him.

This curse was insidious and so much worse than he thought it was. The way the wish had warped and twisted as the curse was unbound was a reflection of the Machiavellian nature of Clodia's mind. She had known the curse could be removed by the right kind of strong enough magic – and Santa's Christmas Wish magic, while unknown to her at the time she lived, was just such magic – so she had obviously ensured there would be horrific consequences to her curse being removed by such magic. Leaving them with the decision to reverse the magic and replace the curse upon Jules and Bas in the cruellest way possible.

She was a hateful bitch. It wasn't enough to know that she had died horribly that night when she'd tried to steal Jules' magic. He wished he could make her suffer in the way she'd made all of them suffer.

But given nobody knew where her soul had gone, that was a wish that could never come true. The only thing he could do was help break the curse.

Which was why he'd been hunting for centuries for clues to where Esta's long-lost diary was as it was the only place he knew of to get the information they needed to break the curse.

Now he had to go back to tracking down the latest lead on it because he had two months to find it and get it in front of Jules. Once the curse was back in place, she would forget everything that she had remembered and experienced in the last few days. As would Bas. Maybe he would too. Maybe it would be better if he did because knowing they had this together and then it was stolen away by him was going to be torture.

But he'd put up with the torture if keeping these memories would mean he could find some way to help them break the curse for good this coming Valentine's Eve.

"Please." Jules' pained voice pulled him back from his spiralling thoughts. "Can someone help with this?"

"Here, let me," Gary said and waved his hand.

SIXTEEN

Jules let out a little scream as what looked like a glass bubble appeared around her, the base of it lifting her off the floor a few inches.

"What the fuck! Jules, are you okay?"

She glanced across the room to see Bas in his own glass bubble – obviously the reason his voice had sounded slightly distant and echoing – hovering right next to the kitchen table. He looked unharmed and seemed to be able to breathe. As could she.

"Jules?"

He sounded so worried. "I'm fine. I promise." She knocked on the glass. "What is this thing?"

Tam made a growling sound as he turned to scowl at the grumpy elf who, with a wave of his hand, had created these giant glass bubbles. "Gary, did you have to snow globe them?"

Gary shrugged. "It's the best way to keep them apart. And it's not like I'm going to snowstorm them like I had to do for Nick and Merry. These two seem to be able to keep control of themselves better than my boss and his wife."

Jules shook her head trying to understand everything the elf – Gary – had just said. She wanted to ask about the snow globe and if she was going to run out of air any time soon, but the question that made it out of her mouth was, "Who are Nick and Merry?"

Gary stared at her as if she had lost her marbles then gestured at the man in the red and white suit – a Santa suit if she wasn't mistaken – who was sitting at the table opposite where Bas hovered in his snow globe, eating fruit cake. While he was dressed up like Santa, he didn't look anything like any Santa she'd ever seen. In fact, he looked more like Hugh Jackman as Wolverine when he was playing at being a logger – but with a snowy beard instead of sexy dark stubble.

Knowing he was Nick didn't help her with who he was. "He's Nick? But who is Nick?"

"Saint Nick. Sinterklaas. Otherwise known as Santa Claus."

"Santa Claus is actually real?" Jules said, gaping at the strapping man through the glass bubble.

"Ho-ho-ho, I certainly am young Julianna," the hot Santa said in a deep, rumbly voice that had happiness bubbling inside her. "Very nice to meet you too. And thanks for the hospitality. Rudolph and I very much appreciate it."

She glanced at the reindeer he gestured to – it raised its head to wink at her, its red nose glowing brightly. She blinked rapidly at him, hardly able to believe her eyes. "You're Rudolph," she said dumbly. It nodded and gestured with his head towards Santa. In her mind she heard, *"And he's Santa."* Then the reindeer returned to the bowl on the floor.

She stared at it for a moment longer before her gaze snapped back to the man it had called Santa. "Y-you look nothing like what I thought Santa looked like – apart from the suit and the beard of course."

"Ho-ho-ho, that's no surprise," he said jovially. "My wife Merry is prone to be a bit jealous and so she put out in the world that I was a fat old man."

"It wasn't truly jealousy. More a quid-pro-quo kind of thing," Gary said. "She said if people saw her as my elf-brethren drew her, then you could be seen in the same way."

"Ho-ho-ho, she did indeed, the cheeky minx. Although you are wrong about the jealousy, Gary. There has never been any talking her into putting out actual images of me – not even when I said I would get the elves to change the images of her too. She just simply didn't want other people lusting after me. I have to say, I'm rather okay with it because it means I can move around the world at other times of the years and people don't notice me at all."

"I rather doubt that," Jules muttered. The man was huge, both in height and muscled shoulder and chest breadth, his biceps and legs were filling out his jacket and pants in a way that the Santa she had always imagined never did. And behind that white beard, he had twinkling blue eyes and chiseled features that would grab attention wherever he went.

She shook her head and pulled her gaze away, looking at the demi-God who Bas had told her was Tam and the elf – Gary – who seemed like they knew what was going on. "Can one of you please tell me what the Hells – sorry Santa —" He waved his hand and continued to eat fruit cake. "Should I call you Santa or Nick? Or maybe Saint Nick?"

He swallowed his mouthful of cake and said, "Either Santa or Nick are fine."

Head spinning that she was actually talking to Santa

Claus, she managed to nod and pull her spiralling thoughts back to her actual question. "Can one of you please tell me what the actual Santa Claus is doing here in my kitchen?"

"As we said before, he's here to help," Tam said, then waved at Gary and Rudolph. "They're all here to help."

"And you're helping us by putting us in these snow globes?" Her gaze flicked between Santa and Gary.

"Hardly," Gary snorted. "It's only a temporary fix. But being in there should have alleviated your urges for now."

Jules frowned as she realised it was true – the need to be with Bas in the most intimate way was still there, but it wasn't pushing her to insane actions like it had been increasingly doing since the curse was broken. "Thanks for the help," she said, smiling at Gary.

His brows shot up in obvious surprise and then turned to Santa, gesturing at her. "You see. That's what gratitude looks like."

"I am always grateful for the help you give me," Santa said. "It's just, you know-ho-ho how I feel about snow-globing people. And I don't particularly love the fact you left Merry trapped in one when we left."

"Well, we couldn't risk her following on one of the other reindeer, or Blitzen when he returned to the North Pole."

"She wouldn't have done that."

Gary raised a sceptical brow. "Really?"

Santa blushed. "Okay, she would have. But that's not the point."

"And what is the point?"

"Ah, I think the point is why you are all here," Bas said loudly, interrupting their argument. "You had only just begun to tell me what is going on after I had fed and scotched Rudolph, and now that Jules is here and you've got us in these ..." he tapped at the globe he was trapped in, "My brain is having a hard time taking in what you've told me already and I heard all of it so far. Jules only came in part way, so I can only imagine how confusing this is for her." He looked between Tamuel, Santa and Gary expectantly. "Can you start at the top, Tamuel?" His gaze flicked to Jules. "For both of us."

"Yes," Tam said, the expression on his face pained. "Of course. Thanks." He cleared his throat. "Well, just after we made our wish and Jules came out of her depression and started to remember and you two—" He coughed. "Well, you know what you two were doing, I left to go down to the library, intending to open a portal to my study. But another portal opened before I could call my magic and Gary and Rudolph here flew out of it." He then went on to give a brief accounting of his trip to the North Pole and what was going on there and what he had been told.

Jules's mouth dropped open as he told his story – for starters, while she loved Christmas and all that came with it, she'd honestly never believed Santa, his reindeer and the elves who helped him were anything more than a myth to help people share the joy of the season. To hear that their North Pole home was real and that were elves and flying reindeer – and all sorts of other magical creatures – living there, as well as Mrs Claus, whose name was Merry, and who would apparently give Jessica Rabbit a run for her money in the sexy siren department, was a lot to take in. Added to that the reason why Gary and Rudolph had kidnapped Tam and taken him there so that they could show him how the broken curse was affecting Santa and his wife – and slowly but surely the rest of the world for that matter – was just blowing her mind.

"Hold on, hold on," she said, hands flattened against

the glass of the globe. "And this is why you have to put the curse back in place?"

Tam flinched but nodded. "Yes. Although, it's not as simple as just rebinding the curse to you and Bas. That's why Santa is here. We have to unbind the Christmas Wish Bas and I made and Santa granted. It's a tricky piece of magic, kind of like winding back time, except without the going back in time bit. It will stay today but things will be returned to how they were before we made the wish."

"And all of this is because the breaking of the curse in this way has made us keep having sex and that sexual need is being channelled to Santa and Mrs Claus?"

"Yes."

"But ..." She shook her head again. "I understand how aggressive emotions can get out of hand and be destructive, but I don't understand how our having sex constantly has affected things so quickly. Or got Santa involved."

"Tam just covered that," Gary said, irritably.

"Explain it again," Bas said. "It takes a bit to get your head around."

She nodded. It did at that.

Tam sighed and said, "Because of a particularly nasty twist in the curse, when it was broken in the way it was, your sexual need rebounded through the wish to Santa and Merry Claus creating a link between you. And because of the way Santa is locked into the spiritual nature of the world at this time of the year, your influence on them – making them behave like you two have been with undying sexual need – is beginning to affect the world in a horribly negative way."

"A way that could destroy everything sooner rather than later?"

"Yes," Gary, Tamuel and Santa said together.

"Can't we just …" She made a cutting gesture, "cut the link between us and Santa? Surely that would give us time to come up with another way to deal with this?"

Gary shook his head. "Nope. As long as the wish is in place, that link will be there. There is no undoing it without undoing the wish."

She blinked back furious tears. "I can't believe this is happening. I mean, I had realised the possibilities of our loving being destructive if it kept on the way it was going, but this?" She shook her head dumbly. "I never thought it would like this. I can't believe our love is so disastrous to the world."

"Our love's not disastrous," Bas said firmly, his stance echoing hers as he faced her, his gaze meeting hers across the space between them, filling her with warmth like it always did. "It is the curse that is causing this. A clause Clodia wove into it to keep us suffering if we tried to break it with the kind of powerful magic that could work outside the confines of curse law."

"Then … if the curse can't be broken with powerful magic like this without something terrible happening, how will it ever be broken?" Fingers of hopelessness reached out, threatening to claw at her. She sucked in a shaky breath, trying to shove them away, but couldn't help asking, "Will we be trapped forever, being together but forever apart like we were? Will you be forced to be a cat during the day and a blind man at night forever?"

Bas shook his head, pressing his hands up harder against the globe, as if he was trying to press through it to get to her. "Not forever. Remember that Tam and I had a plan to break it. We just have to find one more piece of information and then wait until the time of year when the curse was first bound to us."

"Valentine's Eve?"

"That's right," Tam said. "So you won't have long to wait until we manage to break it properly."

"And you'll be able to break it properly? This won't happen again?" She couldn't stand having to go through this again. Having her memories returned to her and her ability to truly love Bas as was always meant to be, only to have it ripped away was not something she wanted to go through now, let alone again. But she couldn't let their love destroy one person, let alone the world.

Tam and Bas nodded.

"They certainly will, ho-ho-ho," Santa said then grimaced as the others turned to glare at him. "Sorry, I do not mean to sound like I think this is funny. It certainly isn't. It's just this time of year affects me in this jolly kind of way. It's part of me putting Christmas Spirit out into the world. I have to feel the ho-ho-ho goodness in every part of me and it's hard for me to turn it off."

"It's fine. I understand." She didn't really. This was all so much to take in, and the fact Santa was apologising for being so jolly just made it all the crazier. He seemed to need her understanding though, and she was happy to give it. Taking a deep, steadying breath, fighting against the claws of hopelessness that were still threatening to sink into her heart, her soul, she asked, "So how do we go about doing this?"

Santa stood. "It's a bit complicated, but basically, Bas and Tam need to make another wish – to undo the first wish. Then I will do what I do and grant that wish, essentially returning things to the way they were before they made the wish."

"Sounds simple."

"It isn't," Gary said. "Not for Santa and certainly not for you."

She turned to face the grim looking elf. "What do you mean? What do I have to do?"

"You have to stay focused and positive, which isn't going to be easy."

"Why?"

"Because as the curse is bound to you again, you will feel it in every part of you. All your memories of when Clodia first spelled the curse will flash to the fore like you are experiencing that moment – and the moments afterwards as you suffocated – as if they are happening. Bas too will experience the same. It will be painful and traumatic and there is nothing we can do to stop it from happening to you."

Jules' lips trembled. She'd experienced that when she had woken that morning and it had been horrible. But she could go through that again if it would save the world. It wasn't truly herself she was worried about. She hated the idea of Bas going through once more what he went through that night. She hadn't seen the moment Clodia had turned him into a cat, but she'd heard his cries of pain and she didn't want him to go through that again. She also didn't want either of them to go through the trauma of losing their son again – particularly as they were yet to find out what happened to him.

Tears filled her eyes. She had so wanted to find him. She'd had so many plans once they were reunited. And now ... now ... it seemed like none of that might happen. Because despite how positive Bas and Tam had sounded about being able to properly break the curse this coming Valentine's Eve, she could read between the lines. There was a chance it wouldn't happen. There was a chance they wouldn't find the information they needed and that they would never be able to meet the rules one needed to break a curse. And there was always the chance Clodia had woven something else into her curse that meant it could never properly be broken because something like this would always happen if they tried.

But she couldn't bring any of that up now. Bas and Tam seemed to need the hope of thinking the curse could be broken and she didn't want to show them her negative thoughts and feelings on the subject.

So she swallowed them back, shoving away those claws of hopelessness. She took a deep shaky breath, and said, "At least I will have my memories of our time together. That will help me to stay positive through it all and keep going."

There was a horrible silence after she spoke. She looked around the room between her love, Tamuel, Santa and Gary. Even Rudolph had lifted his head, his eyes swirling in a way that made her feel like he was sorry for her.

"What?" she asked, the word catching. She cleared her throat and asked huskily, "What aren't you telling me?"

Tam took an unsteady step towards her, his hands raised in a pleading gesture. "I'm so sorry," he said softly. "But when the curse is back in place, you won't remember any of this. You won't remember who you were. You won't remember you love Bas. You won't remember that there is even a curse."

"I'll forget about my son too?" she asked, voice wobbling.

He gasped, his mouth working as he nodded.

"I'm afraid you will, my love," Bas said, his voice achingly sad. "You won't remember anything that's happened in the last day."

"Will you remember?"

He shook his head. "No. Nor will Violetta. And most likely, neither will Tam or anyone else here. It will be as if it never happened."

"We will both return to the state we were in before the wish was made?"

"I—" His gaze went to Tamuel, Gary and Santa.

"That we do not know," Santa said softly.

"But I thought you said my depressive state was beginning to seep out through the ley-lines and were affecting others around us in negative ways? How can we let that happen?"

"It might not happen," Bas said hopefully. "You might not sink back into the depression."

"But you don't know for certain if I will or not?" He shook his head sadly. "Is there no other way?" she asked the others.

"No," Gary said shortly.

"I'm afraid not," Tamuel said more gently, glaring at the elf. "What is happening now is far more destructive than what your depression was causing. And because Santa is involved, it will happen much faster too."

"He's right my dear," Santa said. "We have to stop the repercussion of the rebounding curse from seeping out further into the world and destroying everything."

"But ... if I'm so depressed I can barely function and Bas is heading down that path too, then how will he be able to do what needs to be done to help Tamuel break the curse in the right way? For that matter, how will I – I expect I need to eventually be involved in some way?" She looked around the room at all of them when Bas nodded. None of them seemed able to answer her.

"That is too cruel!" she cried as anger started to burst to

life inside her. Her focus turned to the wish-granting magical man in the room. "Why would you let this happen?" she asked Santa. "I thought you were about spreading goodness and kindness and empathy? What part of this is any of those things?"

Santa shook his head sadly at her as he stood and approached her bubble. "None of them are, my dear. I know it is ho-ho-ho-rribly unfair and I wish there was something I could do. I wish—" He stopped and tipped his head to the side as he turned to look at Rudolph. "I don't think that will help," he said after a moment.

"No," Gary said, stepping forward, hand raised. "I think Rudolph might be right. I think there is a way we can help them over the next few months without affecting the curse in any negative way."

"And how do we do that?" Tam asked hopefully.

"Another wish must be made," Santa said.

Tam frowned. "But how will I be able to do that if I too lose my memory of what has happened here? I won't remember I need to make another wish."

Gary stamped his foot. "Not you, you idiot. Santa. Santa has to make the wish."

"Can he do that?" Bas asked. "I thought he could only grant wishes, not make them."

The elf shook his head impatiently. "No. No. He makes a wish every year. The biggest wish. The most important wish. He makes a wish for happiness, goodness, kindness and empathy to go out into the world and for all of that to last throughout the year. He makes a wish that his Christmas Spirit will continue to affect the world between one Christmas and the next so that there will be people who help their family, friends and neighbours; so that people give charity to those in need; to ensure people will be more likely to try to spread goodness and kindness and empathy than not. All the other wishes that are made and that he grants are nothing to the one that he makes and grants every year. His entire being is given over to creating and granting of that wish – everything else is just prelude to that."

Jules couldn't help but frown more deeply as he spoke, slowly shaking her head. "That's wonderful for the world, but how will that help us?"

"He needs to focus a part of that wish on you and Bas and Tam, ensuring you will be truly imbued with Christmas Spirit that will last beyond the season." Gary turned to stare at Santa. "If he does that, then you will not fall to your depression again. You will celebrate Christmas as you usually do, and the joy you usually feel will help you through the next few months."

"That is all?" Tam asked.

Jules shook her head at him, a slow smile breaking out on her face. "No, Tam. That isn't all. That's everything."

For the first time since she'd walked into the room, the elf lost his grumpy, disapproving visage and smiled back at her. "It's no wonder you were always on the Good List, Julianna Stevens."

"I was?"

"Of course," Santa said fondly.

Gary nodded. "You are not only the smartest person in this room, aside from me of course, but you think that happiness and joy are worth everything. That feeling alone will always set you on the right path. I am certain you would have gotten over your depression in time."

"But not time enough to help us break the curse?"

Gary shook his head. "Probably not. Which is why

Santa will ensure your goodness and happy nature shines through."

"Absolutely," Santa said, chortling and placing his hand up against the glass bubble as if he wished to cup Jules' cheek. "You have put good things out into the world, Julianna Stevens. Now let us give a little bit of that back to you and yours."

SEVENTEEN

"Here, here, elf. I agree she deserves that and more."

Jules turned to see her grandmama walking into the kitchen, edging around the glass globe she was in that almost blocked the entrance.

"You snow-globed them to keep them apart?" she asked as she glanced at Bas in his globe and then centred her attention on the elf.

Gary nodded and crossed his arms belligerently. "I did. And I'm not banishing the globes until the wish is undone."

"And so you shouldn't. Given the phone call I just fielded and the problem that's beginning to grip the world, it's a very clever short-term solution to the problem at hand."

Gary dropped his belligerent pose and looked a little chuffed. "I like her," he said to nobody in particular.

"Thank you." She crossed the room to stand before Santa and held out her hand. "Violetta Stevens. Welcome to Stevens House, Niklaus Kringle."

Santa looked down at her, a slightly bemused expression on his face. "You know who I am without question?"

"Of course. I have been in this world too long to ignore what is plain in front of my face. For Christmas Spirit to last as it does, there needed to be someone behind it. It only made sense that the myth of Santa Claus was a construct to hide a very real, extraordinary, magically gifted Being."

"Ho-ho-ho. I shouldn't be surprised given all I know of you, Violetta Aurelia Stevens." He took her slender hand in his giant one and shook heartily. "I have always been very pleased with the work you've done to keep good and kindness in the world – namely what you have done with your coven, the way you deal with the knowledge you acquire and the most noteworthy of all: what you've done to rear this extraordinary soul who is your granddaughter."

Violetta tipped her head. "Of course. She is an exceptional woman with potential to heal the world if we can only find a way to truly break her curse and free the power that was always meant to be hers."

Bas and Tam gasped. "You know?"

She turned to face them. "I didn't know for certain until now, but I have always suspected. Why do you think I have made it my business to become the foremost expert in the witching world on curses – the making and the breaking of them? It wasn't only because I know you are cursed, Bas, but because there has been the history of a cursed soul weaving in and out of the Stevens lineage for thousands of years. I've never been able to track down the exact curse or who placed it on whom and for what reason, but given the fact my granddaughter is obviously a magical being with no magic, I had come to believe it was because the magic attached to her soul was blocked from her or stolen by a curse of some evil nature. It is what I have been working on with Thomas all these years. I gather that's why you're here." Her gaze pinned Tamuel to the spot. "Although why you would feel the need to play-act as a human who is more my age, I have no idea. I always knew you were something other."

"How do you know it's me?" Tamuel asked, looking not a little flabbergasted. "I don't look a thing like the man I've always shown you."

"Your aura. The pulse of your extraordinary power. It was nothing like I had ever felt in any earth-bound witch. It would have made me wary of you except ... there was something familiar and trustworthy in it. And, you seemed to give Bas here something to work on and look forward to. So I just played along."

"I ... I ..." Tam shook his head.

"We should have known you would not be so easily fooled," Bas said.

"Yes. You should." Violetta's brow rose in the remonstrative way she had of making you feel like a naughty child caught with her hand in the lolly jar. "But what I know and don't know is not the point of why Santa Claus and his cohorts have come to our house this day, is it? It has to do with the curse that's on Bas and Jules. It's the same curse, isn't it?"

"You know that too?" Tamuel choked out.

She waved her hand at him. "I didn't. Not before I saw Saint Nick here and realised what is happening has something to do with their curses being broken. And then I realised one wish couldn't break both curses no matter how powerful the granter." She raised her brows at Santa and he nodded congenially, but didn't add anything to what she was saying. "So, I realised there had to be only one curse, not two. One curse that's bound both of them, that tortured and tormented both of them in different ways. One curse that had been removed in a way it was never meant to be removed and has had a rebound affect as a result. And given it has rebounded in the way it has, the curse had to be one malevolent and powerful working to separate not just two lovers, but two soulmates." Her gaze lit on Bas and then Jules, such empathy and sorrow in her eyes. "It is far worse than I ever realised. I am so sorry I did not see it before now."

"You could not have known, Grandmama."

"I should have. I am the expert in such matters after all."

"No." Tamuel stepped forward and put his hand on her shoulder so that she turned to look at him. "The curse was designed to ensure that others didn't know the link between Bas and Jules. It was actively keeping you from knowing."

Her eyes widened and she gasped. "So I will forget all that I have figured out once you have put it in place?"

He nodded. "I'm afraid you will. I'm afraid all of us will forget all of what has happened these last few days."

"But ..." She turned to Santa. "Is there not something you could do to change that fact? What if I wish—"

"Fuck no!" Gary said, stepping in front of her. "There will be no more wishes outside of the one that Bas and Tam must make to reverse what has been done."

"What about the wish Saint Nicholas must make to ensure Jules keeps her Christmas Spirit?" Bas asked.

"That is a separate thing that lies at the heart of his yearly duties. And it is not a separate wish, but just an adjustment of the wish he makes every moment of every day at this time of year so that a tendril of it specifically touches Jules, and therefore Bas too. Because despite the curse keeping them apart, they are linked forever and always. The curse cannot remove their soul-bond. It is unbreakable."

"And you cannot adjust your wish to ensure we remember?" Violetta asked Santa.

He shook his head. "No-ho-ho, I am very sorry to say, I can't. The curse must be placed on them again and when it is, there is nothing I can do to change the nature of it. It was spelled to punish Bas by making him be the only person who truly remembered and Jules by taking away everything she loved and valued and not allowing her access to them in any reincarnation."

Violetta frowned. "Then why does Tamuel know so much about it?"

Tam's eyes flared wide, panic rushing through him as she blundered so close to the truth.

But then Bas said, "My father Eros arrived not long after and saw what was done. Clodia's curse was not placed on him, so he remembered and he told Tamuel, isn't that right, Tam?"

Tam nodded, thankful that his old lie still rang true and that Bas still believed it. His parents were already about to lose so much, they didn't need to discover who he actually was only to realise they would lose that knowledge too. Right now, he couldn't take the loss either. It would be too much. Too much.

It would be another cruelty that could have lasting effect on them that even Nick's Christmas Spirit wish wouldn't stand up against.

Jules needed her Christmas Spirit intact. Her emotional state affected too many people – and for some reason, it also affected the ley-lines too. He couldn't do anything to put it at risk. Not when this unintended breaking of the curse had failed and their last chance was this coming Valentine's Eve. It was the last one for centuries where everything aligned to replicate the night the curse was placed. They needed the diary to tell them the last pieces of the puzzle – and to also wake Jules up enough once her memory of these things was taken from her again, so that she would be a knowing part of breaking the curse. It was the only way it would work.

Maybe that's why this hadn't worked. Because she hadn't been a part of it. So if they tried again with her a part of the wish – all three of them who had been there when the curse was bound – then maybe they had a chance for the wish to work!

Excitement thrilled through him for a moment and he turned towards Santa to voice his thoughts, but as he did, realisation struck, and his hope and excitement slid away.

Curses had rules, as did the breaking of them. And if the witch who placed the curse wasn't available to unbind it, then everything had to be the same – time, place, people, the placement of the moon and the stars, the magical sigils used. There would always be consequences if the curse was broken any other way. If he hadn't believed that true before, he did so now.

So having Santa grant another wish from the three of them wouldn't work. Not even wishing for them to succeed would work because Santa did not have control over the threads of fate. He only had control over the things that could increase Christmas Spirit and while knowing they'd succeed would increase Tam's happiness, joy and hope – all essential elements of Christmas Spirit – once the curse was in place, his memory would be gone too, so he couldn't remember they would succeed. So the wish would become useless anyway.

No, the only way forward was the one Gary had suggested.

Jules must have Christmas Spirit imbued within her regardless of not remembering her time with Bas. It was the only way to get them all through the next few months.

He focused back in on what was being said. The conversation had continued while he'd been lost in his swirling thoughts and they were still arguing the fact of remembering. He sighed and stepped between Violetta, Gary and Nick. Turning to face Violetta, he said, "It's wasting our time to argue about this. The wish must be wished out of existence, the curse must be re-bound to Jules and Bas exactly as it was with no changes."

"But—"

"But nothing." He held up his hand to stop Violetta – over the last fifty years that he'd been working with her as Thomas the procurer of ancient books, grimoires, scrolls and other magical items that now resided in the Stevens' Library, he'd come to not only respect her, but think of her as a dear friend. He enjoyed the fact she looked at him and accepted his true face – who he truly was – and he hoped that one day soon, she would see him like this again. But that time was not now. Sighing, he put his hand on her shoulder. "You have studied curses for years. You, more than anyone, know the dangers of trying to alter them in any way. We are seeing that danger come to pass right now." He gestured at Jules and Bas and then towards the doors leading outside. "The world is being affected in a bad way because we tried to change things in the wrong way. We can't compound that bit of foolishness by trying to change it again. The only way to get rid of this curse is by continuing down the path we have been on to break it for all these years. We cannot try to hold onto our memories of all this if it might bring more suffering – especially given we know that at the heart of the curse is the wish to cause suffering, and that is what will happen if we don't do this the right way."

Violetta's eyes shone with tears, her lip wobbling. "But ... my granddaughter has suffered so much. As has Bas."

He nodded. "I know. And their suffering must continue for a little longer." As did his. "But we were already on the path towards breaking it the right way and we must continue on it without the knowledge we now have."

"What if we fail?"

"We can't. We won't."

"How do you know?"

"I know," Tamuel said, pressing his fist to his chest. "I know."

"I know too," Bas said. Tam and Violetta turned to stare at Bas. He didn't look at them though – his gaze was centred fully on Jules. "My fate is to be with Jules. To love Jules. To be loved by Jules. No other future can exist but that one. It isn't possible."

Jules nodded as he spoke, her hands splayed up against the glass walls of her snow globe. "No it can't. That is the only future. Our future. I believe it too. More than I've believed in anything else." She tore her gaze from Bas to look at her grandmama. "And you must believe it too," she said softly but firmly. "We cannot return to how things were with any doubts about how things will turn out. We all must believe. We all must have faith that things will turn out the way we want them to."

Violetta sniffed and nodded. "I do. Believe. I want this for you more than I've wanted anything. So I believe."

Santa clapped his hands together, the sound reverberating around the kitchen, making them all jump. "This is fantastic. It will very much help my wish that you are all in such a positive mindset about what lies ahead. I might not be able to ensure you all get what you want – and deserve – but I can ensure you all face it with positivity and focus. And I can ensure that positivity and belief continues to come from the Christmas Spirit that lives in Jules' heart and soul even when things look the bleakest."

"Here-here!" Tamuel heard in his head as Rudolph lifted his impressively racked head and gave a honk of triumph.

"Thanks Rudi. I appreciate the support." Santa patted his reindeer with a loud slap-slap then, ignoring the fact he'd made Rudolph stagger under the force of the gesture, moved into the centre of the room and put his arms out. "Now, it's time to get ready."

"What do we have to do?" Bas asked.

"I need you out of that globe. Gary?"

Gary shook his head. "While you've all been prattling on, I've been keeping track of the sexual energy between them and it has grown, not dissipated, so I'm not sure that's a good idea. It could rush outside and then there'll be orgies in the streets."

"I can increase the shields around the house and this room," Violetta said. Her gaze slid sideways to Tam. "Although, I could do with a magical booster to help hold them for as long as it takes to do whatever Santa here needs to do. I assume it's going to take longer than a minute or two?"

"It will probably take about five to ten minutes to take a hold once I start," Santa said. "But there is also the preparation too, so any shields you put up will need to last for at least twenty minutes if not half an hour."

"Tam, can you help give me the boost?"

"Happy to."

Santa shook his head. "Nope. No-ho-ho can do. I will need Tam to concentrate on wishing the wish to reverse, not to mention he must help me to set up the magical sigils that he and Bas will need to draw on each other and stand within. Gary?" He turned to his elf. "You can help the witch."

"Can I?"

"Certainly. Her shields need help and you can give it to her."

"How?"

"Tell her how you create the snow globes and then bind that magical intent with her shields around it. I think that will do the trick."

"Why don't I just put a snow globe up around the entire house?" Gary asked sarcastically.

Santa clapped his hands again – everyone winced at the boom of sound – and said, "Fantastic idea. You do that and Violetta can strengthen the internals with her shields."

"I ..." Gary mouthed like a fish.

Santa clapped him on the back. "You always come through in a pinch, my friend. Glad I made you come with us today."

"Made me come with you?" Gary squeaked. "I'm the one who—"

"You're the one who what?" Santa asked him, brows raised.

Gary made a face and waved his hand. "Never mind. Come on witch. Let's go and erect the snow globe and strengthen it with your shields. Once that's done, I'll release Bas so that you can get started."

"Ho-ho-ho, good plan," Santa said, slapping him on the back again. Gary stumbled forward, shot a nasty look at his boss, then grabbing Violetta by the arm, edged around

Jules' snow globe and pulled the older witch out the door, leaving the kitchen.

"What can I do?" Jules asked as her grandmama disappeared.

"You can concentrate on all the things about Christmas that make you feel happy and delighted. Fill yourself with those memories and emotions and don't let them go."

"Is that all?" Jules said, hands dropping from the globe to her side. "I wish I could do more than that."

Santa strode across to the globe she stood in, placed his hand on the glass near her face as if he meant to cup her cheek. "Doing what I ask of you is doing more than anyone else here can do. Your positive memories and emotions ... they are going to be one of the biggest helps to me while we unbind this wish and I place my own out into the world, focusing a portion of it on you. Your emotions, memories and good intent is what will make it stick and last."

Jules paled a little. "So everything kind of relies on me being able to hold onto happy memories?"

"In part. But not for one moment do I think you incapable of doing this. I have never met someone who holds Christmas Spirit in their heart as strong and clearly as you do for the entire year. You are precisely the reason I exist to do what I do. You are my inspiration and my reason for being. It is people like you who make all the sacrifices of my energy and time worth it. Just be who you are meant to be, Jules. That's all I ask of you. That's all anyone can ever ask of you."

Her mouth twisted and she nodded. "That is one of the nicest things anyone has ever said to me."

"Every word is true." He turned and waved his hand at the others in the room. "They will all vouch for that."

"Believe in yourself, my love," Bas said. "Because we all do."

"You do?" Tears thickened her voice.

"Absolutely," Tamuel said, feeling a bit emotional himself.

In his mind he heard, *"Ditto."* Looking around he saw that everyone else had heard Rudolph as well.

Santa beamed at all of them and then clapped his hands again, the boom ringing around the room. "Fabulous. This will help too. This love and trust you all have for each other. Keep that up." He pointed at Jules. "Now, start filling yourself up with Christmas Spirit memories while Tam, Rudolph and I get the circle ready."

As he joined Santa to listen to the instructions the big, jolly, handsome man was giving him and Rudolph, he couldn't help but notice Jules and Bas staring at each other. Their hands were up against the glass bubbles they were trapped in, pressing hard as if they were aching to touch the other – they probably were. Then Bas mouthed, "I love you. I have faith in you."

Jules nodded, a tear running down her cheek as a smile broke out on her lips. "I love you too. I have faith in you too." Then she closed her eyes and did what Santa bid her to do.

He knew she was doing it, because despite the barrier of the globe, Tam suddenly felt happier and more hopeful than he'd felt since Gary had kidnapped him and took him to the North Pole.

CHAPTER

EIGHTEEN

Bas couldn't believe he was doing this. Taking away his and Jules' happiness when it was all he'd fought for over the last few thousand years since Clodia's evil had ripped away from them simply because she wanted the Goddess powers that Jules had been blessed with at birth.

It hadn't been much of a blessing, truth be told. If Julianna had never been gifted those powers by Vesta, she would never have grabbed the attention of Clodia in the first place; she would never have been taken by Clodia to become a Vestal Virgin so the priestess could use those powers while Julianna was a child, and if she had never been forced into the life of a Vestal Virgin, their love affair would never have been forbidden and considered a crime against the state of *Roma*. Those powers had never done Julianna any favours – and given he was fated to be her mate, they'd never done him any favours either. Or their son.

Sadness engulfed him at the thought that he still didn't know what had happened to their son. He assumed that he would be a cupid due to the fact he was Bas' son, but his father had completely ignored him ever since he was cursed, so he had been unable to ask. He was obviously *persona non grata* as far as Eros was concerned. Not only had he dared to fall in love and have a child, but he had committed a worse crime by allowing himself to be cursed by a witch. He'd asked Tamuel early on when he realised he could trust the cupid, but he hadn't known anything. Eros had either taken his child as was his right as leader of all cupids, and was hiding the child's heritage from everyone, or he had ignored his existence altogether.

There might never be any way of finding out what had happened to the boy.

"There. Is that right?"

Bas looked up at Tamuel who stood in front of him, a gold-speckled paint brush in his hand. If he had one wish about his son it was that he was happy. If he had another it would be that he was someone like Tamuel – kind, empathetic, caring and always concerned about other people's happiness. He was the best of what a cupid could be. If his son was even half the man Tamuel was, then he would be proud of him.

Suddenly Santa was there in front of him too, leaning in closely to peer at Bas' naked chest. He pointed just under his collarbone. "You missed a dash there." He pointed at the paper in Tam's hand. "See."

"Oh, yes." The young cupid dipped the paint brush in the sparkly gold paint and then leaned in to add the dash. Bas held still as the warm wetness was brushed across his flesh. "Is that right?"

"Perfect." Santa stood back and said, "Stand still both of you while I make certain you've not missed anything." He did a slow circle around Tamuel and Bas as they stood still, looking at the sigils they'd drawn on each other's skin – their legs, arms, stomachs, chests, backs, necks and faces all had sigils painted on them.

Once he'd been released from the globe – only after Gary had come back to say he'd placed a large snow globe around the house and that Violetta was just finishing with the reinforcing shields – Bas had followed Santa's drawn instructions and had painted them on Tamuel first with the sparkling gold, silver, red and green paint Santa had pulled out of his big red sack along with the magical paint brushes. Then he'd stood still while Tamuel painted them on him – the strangest sensation like wet feathers being drawn across his skin mixed with the tingle of the finest and most delicate magic he'd ever felt before. It was hard to stand still under such a strange, almost tickling sensation that made his skin shiver and prickle and filled him with an excess of energy that grew and grew. He had to force himself not to move a muscle though because, according to Santa, the sigils had to be exact.

Santa had also said it was important that they do the painting because they were the ones unbinding the wish. The sigils themselves were a mix of runes, as well as some kind of ancient Elvish language Santa had learned from Gary's mother – so he'd told them as he worked – and Christmas-centric images like Christmas trees, baubles, stars, bells and boxes with bows on them. As they'd painted the sigils, Santa had taken care of painting the circle and its sigils that they must stand within when they unbound their wish.

Behind Bas, Jules was still trapped in her snow globe. Every part of him hated the fact she was locked in there, but it was necessary. Every second the need pushed at him to go over there and bash on the glass of the globe, to break into it and be with her in the way they longed to be together. But he fought it because giving in would only infect the others in the house and put further strain on the protections Gary and Violetta had placed around the old mansion – protections that were already being strained to contain the energies that seeped out of him and Jules without any conscious thought on their behalf.

The few times he'd allowed himself to glance at Jules, it was easy to see that she was under the same strain as him – at least, easy for him because he knew her so well. To anyone who didn't know her well, she probably looked like she was meditating peacefully. She stood inside her globe, eyes closed as she followed Santa's instructions to fill herself with all the Christmas Spirit memories and feelings she could. But her hands were pressed into her legs, clenching against her thighs occasionally and her jaw was clenched in a way that told him she was fighting the urge to bash her way through the globe to get to him now he was out of his protective globe and there was less of a barrier separating them, helping to hold the insane need at bay.

Violetta re-entered the room soon after Gary did and he couldn't help his gaze following her as she went straight over to stand beside Jules' globe. She placed her hand on the glass and closed her eyes, muttering the words of a shielding spell to try to help Jules in her task. Ever grateful that Violetta had been born into the Stevens family – she had been such a godsend to him at a time when he had begun to lose hope; a friend and the only Stevens family member for many centuries who realised not just that he'd been cursed, but had tried to find a way to undo said curse – he was even more grateful now for the support she always gave her granddaughter, and was continuing to give her, even though the amount of magic she was expending through all the shielding must be costing her a great deal.

Once this was done, he would have to make sure she rested up properly over the next few days. Except ... he wouldn't remember any of this, so wouldn't remember that she'd used up so much magic and energy to help them set things to rights.

Well, not to rights. The only way things would ever be right was when the curse was properly broken and he and Jules could be together in a normal soulmates kind of way.

"That's enough of that," Santa said, appearing in front of him, blocking his view of Violetta and Jules. He tapped Bas' nose in a way that was oddly parental, especially coming from such a strappingly handsome man who, despite his white hair and beard, looked to be in his mid-thirties.

Bas blinked and frowned. "What's enough?"

"You know very well. You were letting your thoughts spiral into darkness again. We can't have any of that. Your Jules ..." He pointed over his shoulder, "is doing one hell of a job in keeping her mind on only positive things. You need to match her for this to work. Because if any sliver of negativity slides into the room while I am placing my wish, then it will invade the wish. And you don't want to see what happens when that occurs. Let's just say a few wars would never have occurred if someone hadn't been in the room with me having a negative thought while I wished my wish for the world."

Bas' brows rose. "Holy shit. Really?"

"Really," Gary said. "It's why we created a wish room for Santa and I built him a special one-way globe to go around his designer chair so he can cast his magics on the world without negative interference. To be doubly secure, nobody is allowed in that room while he's working his magical wish. We have a monitor outside the room so we can see if he's in his chair or not and know not to enter during that time." He sighed and frowned. "It's not great that he's going to be spending part of his wishing time in this room with all of you, but it can't be helped because of what you did. But you all need to make certain you keep only positive thoughts and feelings in your hearts and minds while the wish is being made. Because even the globe I will put him in when he makes the wish here won't stop any negativity from affecting the wish as it seeps out into the world."

"Why can't you put him in the kind of globe you made for him at the North Pole?"

Gary sighed heavily and shook his head. "The kind of magic I used on his globe at home takes time and energy I simply don't have right now. Not even the best globe I can put him in now will keep him safe from insidious negativity." He jabbed his finger at each of them. "So keep your thoughts and emotions in check because I don't want to have to clean up your messes again. Once is enough!" With that he harrumphed and went over to where Rudolph stood and began to paint sigils on the reindeer's body – apparently the reindeer must join them in the circle although the details of why still hadn't been explained to him.

He supposed they would tell them when they got to that moment. Which was fast approaching.

He swallowed back the panic and pain that rose like a wave inside him at the thought that very soon his time with Jules, making love to her, sharing love with her, would be stolen away again. Santa's head snapped up and he angled him a disapproving look and opened his mouth.

Bas raised his hand. "I know. I'll contain it. It's just hard not to think of what I'm about to lose."

"Concentrate on what you will gain in a couple of months when you break the curse properly. Put your good thoughts towards that – your hope and faith that it can be done, that you *will* do it, that you both deserve for it to work – and send them out into the world. If you put good things out into the world, they will come back to you."

"They haven't so far."

"Ah-ah-ah, none of that," Gary turned and waggled the paint brush at him. "The good doesn't come when you want it to or think you deserve it to. It comes when it's most needed. For you and Jules it will come. I am certain of that. As is everyone else in this room."

"*Too right,*" he heard in his head. He stared at Rudolph as the reindeer swung his head around so he could glare at Bas, his red nose pulsing faster. "*Stop focusing on your glums. Good things have happened amongst the bad, cupid. The younger cupid and Violetta came into your life at just the right time. Think about that and like things and not about the stuff in-between. Besides, you were lucky enough to have a great love – she is still in your life even though it's not exactly in the way you would like – and she is your best friend. Some people never get to experience what it is like to have either. So stop being a negative-Nelly and focus on all the luck of having these people in your life.*"

"Well said, Rudi," Santa said.

Bas blinked at the reindeer as Rudolph turned around and said to Gary through mind-speech, "*You missed a Christmas tree topper.*"

"Where?"

"*The one on my left arse cheek.*"

As Gary trotted around the reindeer's flank to check, a

light and slightly echoing voice said, "Concentrate on the love we still feel for each other, my love."

He whipped around to see Jules had opened her eyes, her hand up against the glass of the globe as if she longed to touch him. It took everything in him not to go to her, but he held on, staying where he was, hands clenched tight at his sides. "Jules."

She smiled sweetly at him. "Rudolph is right and it was stupid and selfish of me to ever forget that and allow myself to sink into such a bad depression. We might be cursed, but we have so much that is good in our lives, especially the people who are here for us and will always be here for us. We have our friendship which will last forever. And we have our love."

"We won't remember our love."

"No. Maybe not consciously. But I think I have felt it there since I became old enough to understand such an emotion. I might not have realised what it was in my conscious mind, but it was there supporting me, comforting me, making me feel like I was never alone. That will still be there for both of us. I have faith in it. And it has been strengthened by our loving over the last day. Even if it hadn't, our love has been strong enough to last all this time. It will be strong enough to last through whatever comes next. I love you. You love me. Whether I remember it or not, that will never change. Clodia's curse cannot take that away from us. Not unless we let it. So don't let it. Okay?"

He nodded, his smile blooming to match hers.

Goddess he was so handsome. Even if he wasn't standing there in only his Calvins, his muscled body glistening with the sparkling gold, silver, green and red magical paint, he was the most handsome man she'd ever known. He would always be the most handsome man she'd ever know.

Her fingers flexed against the glass as she once again fought the urge to press up against it sinuously, trying to push herself through it to get to him. But the need didn't control her. She wouldn't let it. Just like she wouldn't let the curse control her in the ways that truly mattered. It didn't control the way she approached the world. It didn't control the way she loved learning and researching and being a Librarian for her family. It didn't control her love for her grandmama or for her best friend. It didn't control the goodness she always wanted to put out into the world.

She filled herself with the knowledge of that, taking in his smile, in the way he looked at her with such love and trust in his eyes. That is what she would hold in her mind as the wish was undone and the curse snapped back into place. And that is what she would never truly forget – not in the deepest heart of her, not in her soul.

She would always feel what Bas was to her in those places – would always feel what she was to him. And it would give her what she needed to get through the next few months. And while Santa was making his wish, she would make her own:

That Bas would remember that too. And that they would succeed – that the curse would be broken and they would be together once again in a more normal way this time without the insane sexual need driving them to act out of character.

It was all she'd ever longed for. It was what she would get. There was no other option.

"Very good, Jules," Santa bellowed, standing up from making the finishing touches on the circle to face her. "You are all I knew you were. You will be the perfect focal point for my wish."

She nodded, chin wobbling. Santa believed in her too. She was glad she'd always believed in him – if not in the actual real-life magical Being, she had believed in the spirit he embodied. She would grasp a hold of that spirit and not let go. "Thank you. I will do my best not to let you or the world down."

"I know you will, my dearest girl," he said, beaming widely as he met her gaze. Then his gaze flickered to Violetta. "You have raised a remarkable woman."

"I know," Violetta said, hand tapping on the glass of the globe.

Jules reached sideways and splayed her hand against the glass where Violetta's hand was splayed. She smiled at her grandmama who smiled back with all the love and trust she'd ever had for Jules in her eyes.

It filled Jules with such a sense of being loved – she even felt the love coming from Tamuel who was smiling mistily at her too, as well as a little bit from Gary and Rudolph, and Santa of course. That love ... it was everything.

And it would see her through whatever was to come.

"Feel what I feel through our bond, my beloved Bas," she said, returning her attention to her mate. "And hold it to you as we do this."

He nodded, eyes full of his love for her, his trust in her. "I will."

"Ho-ho-ho, this is excellent," Santa said. "Are you done, Gary? With all this love and trust and goodness in the room, it's time to get started."

"All done," Gary said, standing back to look over his work. "Time to take your place centre stage, Rudolph."

Rudolph trotted forward into the circle of sigils and

Christmas images that Santa had painted on the floor. Then lowering his head, he said in his echoing mind-speech, *"Bas and Tam, each of you take a point of my rack in your hands just above the painted doves, then complete the circle by clasping each other's hands."*

They did as bid.

"Very good," Santa said, standing close to the circle. "Now stand very still and do exactly as I say. As the magic lifts from your skin, it will feel uncomfortable, but you must stay still and in the circle – and don't let go of Rudolph's rack whatever you do. He will be the thing that will keep you grounded and stop your magic from being sucked away with the wish magic."

Jules frowned. They hadn't previously said there was a chance Bas and Tam's magic could be affected by what they were doing. But neither male seemed surprised, so they must have known and didn't seem phased by it.

Not that they had a choice. They had to do this. Now.

"Are you ready?" Santa asked.

"Ready," they all said one after the other as his gaze lit on them.

"Then let's do this. Gary, the snow globe please."

Gary waved his hands and suddenly Santa was floating a few inches above the ground in his very own snow globe that glistened with gold, silver, red and green lights – it was breathtakingly beautiful.

She had to drag her gaze off it as Santa said, his voice echoing mystically, "Now, listen very carefully and do exactly what I say when I say it. There is no room for mistakes from this point."

Bas and Tam nodded their heads, hands grasping Rudolph's rack more tightly.

"Ho-ho-ho. Let's begin." Santa clapped his hands together, louder than he'd ever done before.

As the sound echoed around the room like a thunder-clap, the painted sigils and Christmas images began to raise from the floor to swirl around the two males and Rudolph within the circle.

"Now, start chanting the wish unbinding, boys, using the exact words we discussed."

As they did so, Jules felt a chill race through her. But before panic could raise its ugly head, Violetta said, "Feel the love. Hold onto the love, my dear."

She took a deep breath and concentrated on doing exactly that.

As she lost sight of Bas and Tam within the circle – the painted sigils and images had lifted from their skin and from Rudolph's and was swirling around in the circle they stood in, like a tornado painted in streaks of gold and silver, green and red, obscuring her view of them. But Santa didn't seem worried. Neither did Gary who stood beside Santa's globe with his hands on the glass. They were both smiling. In fact, they looked like they were filled with joy. A joy that was glowing out of them in a visible way with waves of the same gold, silver, red and green that was swirling around in the circle.

"Very good," Santa bellowed, before giving more instructions that she couldn't quite hear – there was suddenly so much noise in the room. Bells chiming, carols filling the air, reindeer hooves clopping, laughter and the joyous sound of children's excitement. It washed over her, through her, filling her, making it so easy to think of only the good things. "That's it, Jules. That's it. Take it in. Take it all in."

Santa's voice chanted in her head. She could barely see

anything now – brilliant glowing light filled with Christmas colour shone in her eyes, getting brighter and brighter. It filled her with such happiness; with a sense of joy that had been sorely missing lately. It was so glorious, she barely felt the moment something was torn from her, a heaviness threatening to push her down, down in the swirling darkness of the evil it was born from.

But she wouldn't let it take her down. Not now. Not at this time of the year. Not when there was so much to be thankful for.

She had her home.

She had her charities she loved working for.

She had the job that filled her with so much purpose.

She had the love and support of her grandmama.

And she had the wonder of a best friend who would never leave her side, ever.

She was truly blessed.

And thankful for it. And nothing was going to get her down.

"It's done." The voice chimed through her head, but she didn't really register it.

Nor did she truly register another voice as it said, "I'll return this place to how it was and get them all back to their rooms to sleep. Although what should I do with Tam?"

"Return him to the library. It's where he often goes when he needs to find courage in the task before him. There's a couch down there he often sleeps on when nobody else is up."

"Very well. You better get back to the North Pole, Nick. Merry will be waiting."

"I will. But not before I've done something to make this house feel more like it usually does at this time of the year.

That will be my extra gift to Jules and her family. A Christmas they will never forget."

"You are spoiling her."

"Rubbish. The girl deserves a little spoiling. Don't you think?"

An aggravated sigh. "Very well. I'll keep Jules in the globe to protect her from your magic now the curse and her magical allergy is back. And I'll put a little memory inside their minds so they each think the other has done the decorating and the cooking. And so they don't ask each other who did it."

"Ho-ho-ho. What would I do without you, Gary?"

"Your life would be a disaster."

Jolly laughter filled the air as Jules drifted off into a happy sleep dreaming of Santa and reindeer and an elf who was cutely scowly and probably needed a hug.

CHAPTER

NINETEEN

The last twelve days had been mayhem, but everything was finally done and ready for today. Jules had no idea why on earth she had put everything off until so late, nor why she hadn't had this idea earlier, but whatever had got into her mind was gone and she was full speed ahead to the best Christmas Day she'd ever had.

Her smile was so wide it felt like it might fall off the sides of her face as she walked around the house doing a final check of all the items on her clipboard.

Decorations – colourful and plentiful ✓

Lights – twinkling happily ✓

Carols – filling the house with beautiful sounds but not so much one couldn't talk over them ✓

Christmas trees – decorated and at least two per room ✓

Presents for all their guests – wrapped and piled under each Christmas tree ✓

Entranceway to the underground Stevens' Library blocked from access by the public ✓

Stairway to the private parts of the house blocked off✓

Mistletoe – hung in half the doorways for those who wished an excuse for a little Christmas sanctioned PDA✓

Food – plentiful and on the tables in each room with plates, knives, forks and serviettes✓

Drinks – same as food✓

Scent in the house – cinnamon and spices from the freshly baked goodies with a hint of fresh pine✓

Santa hats and reindeer ears – enough for everyone coming with a couple dozen to share, on the tables by the door for guests to grab when they arrive✓

She picked up one of the Santa hats and put it on her head, checking her reflection in the mirror on the wall by the front door. She adjusted the angle and how the pom-pom fell and tucked her hair behind her ears.

There. Perfect.

As was the gorgeous Christmas dress she'd bought to wear today – red and green with gold and silver sparkles scattered across the bodice and skirt in a way that made them look like stars. The sleeves were short and hung loose in a swishy kind of way that echoed the cut and fall of the skirt which fell just below her knees. She'd found gold strappy low-heeled sandals to match that would be comfortable to wear all day.

But the *pièce de résistance* that set the whole thing off was Bas' gift to her.

He'd left it for her under the little Christmas tree she kept on the dresser in her room with a note she was to open it without him. And she was so glad she had as it was a pretty Christmas necklace with matching earrings and bracelet just perfect for her outfit today. The necklace and earrings were tiny gold Christmas trees linked with a fine gold chain, sparkling with the colours of the jewelled baubles set into the branches of the trees. The Christmas trees on the bracelet were set like charms in a charm bracelet, and tinkled against each other when she moved her wrist.

The necklace sat at the base of her throat, delicate and lovely, and the bracelet and earrings sparkled on her lobes and wrist. A little light make-up and red-tinged lip-gloss finished off the look.

She felt pretty and couldn't help smiling at herself as she swished her skirt in front of the long mirror.

It was going to be a glorious day. She could feel it in her bones.

She only wished Bas could stand beside her and enjoy it with her in his human form. But his curse meant that he had returned to his cat form at dawn and he wouldn't change back until sunset. He would be able to enjoy the evening celebrations with her though after he'd recovered from his change – at least there was that. And during the day she'd have her shadow standing beside her – his black cat form – offering her support with his presence. It wasn't what she wished for him – for either of them – but it was better than nothing.

She had to be happy that she had such a wonderful friend in her life despite the fact it wasn't in the most ideal way possible. Especially for Bas.

After Christmas was over, she'd have to redouble her efforts to help her grandmama find a way to undo his curse. He didn't deserve what the curse did to him. Nobody did, but someone so wonderful certainly didn't.

She wished she wasn't so useless where the magical elements of research were concerned. It made thing so much harder because there were so many books and materials in the library she couldn't touch. But she could at least help in the search for what her grandmama could read even though Jules couldn't read at least half of it herself. She sighed. It wasn't easy being the only non-magical person in such a strongly magical family – even worse that she was allergic to magic with the allergy only getting worse as the years passed. Sometimes it was hard to stay positive. It was—

Lights twinkled all around her and a life size Santa in the corner let out a loud 'Ho-ho-ho!' It brought her out of her darkening thoughts and back into the moment. A moment filled with hope and the joy of knowing she had done something that would bring a lot of people happiness today. And full bellies. And a feeling that they were important to somebody.

The sound of buses driving up the drive came through the door and she peered out of the glass on either side of the door. "They're here!"

"No need to bellow, dear," Violetta said, sailing down the sweep of stairs in the centre of the entrance hallway, Bas trotting down the steps at her heel.

He was obviously fully recovered from his change at sunrise. Those changes seemed to be getting a little harder on him – and they were hard enough already – taking him longer to recover once the change was complete.

He left Violetta and raced down the remaining stairs to wind around Jules' feet, brushing up against the bare skin of her legs and meowing up to her loudly.

Laughing, she bent down and picked him up, rubbing her face against the back of his head before giving him a kiss. "I know. I'm excited too. Let's do it, shall we?"

He meowed back at her and gave her hand a lick before

looking pointedly at her necklace. He rarely licked her like that – even though he was a cat from sunrise to sunset, he still mostly kept his human sensibilities. But when he did give in to his cat nature in such a way to show her affection and friendship in the only ways he could in this form, it was extra special – and today even more so. Like a little extra gift after the gorgeous jewellery he'd gifted her early this morning just before he'd gone to his room and locked himself in his shifting pod to protect her from the magic of his change.

She touched the necklace. "I love your gift. It's perfect and so special." She moved her head, showing off the earrings and then jangled the bracelet so that it made a little shifting chiming sound as the Christmas trees jangled against each other. "They make me feel so special. I don't want to ever take them off."

Bas meowed happily and began to purr loudly as she placed him back on the floor.

"They'll be less special if you wear them every day," Violetta said as she joined Jules and Bas. "Better just to keep them for the times you need a little happiness boost."

Jules shrugged. "Maybe. I'll see." She gestured at the door. "Shall we?"

"Absolutely. Let's invite our guests inside." She reached for the door and opened both sides of the entrance wide, a huge welcoming smile on her face as she looked out at the people already waiting on the porch, more trailing up the pathway that led from the sweeping drive where buses had pulled up to disgorge their passengers. "Welcome to Stevens House," she said loudly, her voice carrying across the noise of chatting and the carols that were piped outside the house. "My granddaughter Jules and I are thrilled you are able to join us for our Christmas Day celebrations. Come in, come in."

Children rushed forward with their mothers entering more tentatively behind them. Today was a day for at-risk mothers and their children who were escaping domestic violence – Jules had reached out to so many charities in the last twelve days to organise for them to bring the women and children they worked hard to protect. Women and children who had nowhere else to go and would otherwise have spent an uncertain day that was less than cheering as so many of the charities that helped and housed them didn't have enough money to put on a proper Christmas Day celebration.

Tomorrow they had a day dedicated to young homeless. The day after was for struggling families. In fact, they had something organised every day for different charities right through until – and including – New Years Day. She was also organising online auctions – a suggestion Bas had made and had set up and had done much of the organising when he was in his human form during the night – to raise money for each charity.

It made her so happy to be able to help people like this. It seemed ridiculous to complain about her magical allergy when people were truly suffering. And while she was only giving each of these groups one day of specialness each, she hoped to be able to do more for them by continuing to raise the money they needed to truly help those who needed it.

Seeing the joy on the kids' faces as they entered, and those who were running up the front path, pointing at all the decorations on the lawns outside – the life-size replicas of Santa's reindeer and Santa with his sleigh that sat on the right side of the lawn; the automated elf statues with their happy smiles and red cheeks lining the pathways welcoming the visitors; the sparkling light-covered kangaroos and emus on the lawn on the left side of the path and all the lights that were sparkling all over the front of the huge house – dulled by the daylight but still impressive. She couldn't wait to lead them out the back after dusk to see the lights through the back garden and then see their faces as the fireworks went off.

She had many special things planned for them during the day though before they got there and she couldn't wait.

She, Violetta and Bas greeted every single person as they came in the door, giving them their special Christmas name badge and the gift bag for each of these mothers filled with a little something special – some beautiful cleansers and facial and hand creams, vouchers for massages and a bracelet with a heart and a snowflake on it, each of the snowflakes different as a celebration of each woman's difference. It was really important to Jules that they each knew they were special in their own way and that that should be celebrated.

Other volunteers – some Stevens cousins they'd roped in and a few friends of her grandmama's – were there to guide the visitors inside after they had been greeted at the door, putting the kids into groups to be taken through, once everyone had arrived, to the Christmas trees and presents that were meant for them. That was another thing Bas had helped with – compiling a list of all the kids who were coming and finding out a few special gifts that would delight each of them individually. It had been a lot of work and he'd worked hard through each night, managing everything like a champ with only a few things that needed to be done by her each day – things he couldn't do because of the time he was in his human form and the fact he was blind and not everything could be fixed with voice activated software and Braille technology.

She actually had loved working with him on these things. He'd always helped her with everything she'd thrown herself at, but this last week he had been a Godsend. Although, maybe given the time of the year it was, he was more of a Santasend!

She giggled internally at the name she'd just made up, looking forward to when she could share that thought with him later, knowing he'd laugh too. She loved his laugh. It always warmed her day.

She looked down briefly at her friend as he wound around the legs of a particularly shy little boy who was hiding behind his mother's skirts – they were the last ones to arrive. The little boy looked down at the cat, longing on his face as Bas brushed up against his legs and meowed up at him.

Jules bent down and said softly. "He wants you to pick him up." The little boy looked up at her with such longing in his eyes, then, keeping his gaze on her as if waiting for the moment she might change her mind, bent and picked up a purring Bas, holding the black cat against his chest as if he was the most precious thing.

His mother made a sound – halfway between a sob and a laugh – and Jules looked up at her. The mother leaned close to her and said, "His father killed the old cat I'd brought into the marriage with me. Ben loved that cat so much. When he cried, my ex hit him and told him not to be a baby." A tear fell down her cheek and she swiped it away and sucked in a shaky breath. "It's what made me finally leave him. But it's been so hard ever since." She straightened her shoulders and looked Jules in the eye. "You've no idea what this day means to us. Ben has been looking forward to it ever since we got the invite four days ago. He's talked about it non-stop."

Jules smiled at her and gripped her hand. "Well, I hope you have a wonderful day. And maybe, when you're ready, you will let me help you adopt a kitten or a cat for Ben. But only when you're ready."

"Oh, he would love that but ... are you sure? I don't want to take up too much of your time."

"I'm happy to bring a boy and a pet together. All children need a pet best friend. Bas has certainly been a treasure for me. I'd like to see all children share the kind of special friendship as the one I have." Of course, hers was a little different from the usual pet-human relationship as Bas wasn't her pet, but was a member of her family and her best friend – both in human and cat form – but she couldn't tell this woman that.

The woman's eyes lit up and she gripped Jules' hand hard. "You are such an angel."

"No, you are," she said. "Go with your boy. Enjoy your day."

"I will. I will."

Beaming after the mother who hurried after her son, a spring in her step now as she followed him and the group they were with into the lounge room for the present unwrapping, Jules knew that she would. That everyone here would have not only the best day but begin to hope for many more days like this in their future. She would fill them all with so much Christmas Spirit today that it would last longer than today.

She would make sure of it.

And maybe, just maybe, giving them all hope for a better future would help her to hold onto the hope that there would be a better future for everyone in the world who suffered in some way.

Including Bas. Especially Bas. She vowed in this moment to do everything she could to stop his suffering.

She would find some way to break his curse.

IT WAS JUST after eight and everyone had settled down to eat their late dinner before Jules would lead them outside for the lights and fireworks display she'd organised for their enjoyment as soon as twilight was over and it was dark enough.

Bas sat back to watch the children who'd already eaten and were now playing with the toys they'd been gifted while their mothers sat at the tables and ate the Christmas feast and drank the cocktails and other drinks prepared for them.

He felt the moment Jules walked into the room behind him and he turned to watch her.

She moved between the tables, stopping often to talk to the women, checking on the kids, making certain everyone had everything they could need and were being taken care of. Her happiness exuded from her, touching everyone around her, lifting up those she talked to, those she touched with a gentle, caring hand. It surrounded him where he sat on the back of the lounge, filling him with hope and warmth and, at the same time, making him feel like she was giving him a hug.

And all that without a hint of magic.

She was extraordinary. He was so lucky to have her in his life, even if it wasn't in the way he had longed for over the centuries since the curse had been thrust upon them.

But despite his happiness in this moment, he still longed to be with her as they were always meant to be.

Lovers.

Soulmates.

He longed too to find their son.

He had begun to think maybe it might never happen, despite all the help he'd had in the last century, first from Tamuel and then from Violetta when she realised he was under a curse. But today – this last twelve days actually – he had begun to hope again.

Given he hadn't felt the tingle that said the change was coming as sunset got underway, he stayed longer to enjoy the day, trying to ignore the worry that was creeping in because of the fact he wasn't feeling the pull of the change yet.

His time as a cat seemed to be getting longer over the last few months. Of course, it always was longer at this time of the year given it was summer and daylight savings, which was perhaps why he hadn't noticed it at first. To begin with the difference had been counted in seconds. But then seconds had turned to minutes and now it was becoming noticeably longer. So far Jules hadn't noticed – he'd hidden it from her, saying it was taking him longer to get over the change to explain the extra time he spent away from her. It wasn't completely a lie. The change was taking more from him.

Twilight was turning the night outside purple when the change magic finally pulled at him. Strongly. More suddenly than it usually did. He always had more warning in the past – a tingling that started well before the change did.

He saw Jules frown and shift uncomfortably where she stood across the room watching the children play with their toys. Damn, the magic was starting to reach her. He had to go upstairs and get into his changing booth so she wouldn't be affected even more. Not to mention, none of these humans could become aware that they lived in a world of magic and magical Beings.

He jumped off the couch and raced out of the room, darting around the barrier at the base of the stairs and raced up the sweeping steps and then down the hallway that led to the wing where his and Jules' rooms were. He darted inside his room, leaping into the specially designed glass-sided booth that was in the corner of his suite and shoved the door closed behind him just as the change began to do more than prickle over his skin.

Soon he was lying on the floor, writhing in agony as the change took him apart and put him back together again in his human form. It always felt like it lasted forever but now it felt like it was even longer. As he flipped over onto his back, trying not to scream as his spine broke and reshaped, he saw the clock on the wall. It *was* taking longer. Twenty minutes had already passed and it would normally only take ten minutes at the most.

Sometime later, he lay on the floor, sweat-soaked and aching, his muscles twitching as the change magic finally faded away. The door to his cubicle opened and Tam was suddenly there placing a soft blanket over Bas' naked form. The blanket was light and warm and felt wonderful against his skin which felt like it had been scraped raw.

"Thank you," he managed through a throat that also felt scraped raw. "You didn't let Jules see you, did you? Or Violetta?"

"In this form? Of course not."

Bas winced as his muscles cramped again.

"It's getting worse, isn't it?"

Bas managed to nod as Tam helped him to sit up and lean against the glass walls of the booth. He disappeared briefly only to return a moment later with a glass of juice.

"Here. This will make you feel better." He helped Bas hold the glass to his lips so he could take a sip. "Does Jules know?"

Bas shook his head, swallowed down a mouthful of the juice before saying, "And I don't want her to know."

"She'll figure it out soon."

"I know. But let's keep that worry away from her for as long as possible. She's got her own worries. Not to mention, she has so much on her plate right now helping all the people she wants to help."

"It's quite special what she is doing for all of those people."

"It is."

"She could do more if she had her magic."

"She could."

"We need to break this curse."

"Yes."

"This Valentine's Eve."

"This Valentine's Eve," Bas repeated. "If we find that diary."

Tam met his gaze, his own full of his resolve. "I have a new lead on the diary. More promising than any before. That's what I came to tell you."

"You do? Are you certain this time?"

Tam nodded, his expression grimly determined. "As certain as I can be. I will find the diary and get it into Jules' hands in time. I vow it on the Spirit of Christmas."

"The Spirit of Christmas?"

"The most powerful magic at this time of the year. Look what it helps Jules do despite the fact she can't be around magic. There is something truly magical and special about it. And I think the Spirit of Christmas and its magic is going to help us to succeed. Don't ask me how I know. I just know it."

"Then I vow on it too."

The two cupids shook hands, both vowing they would use everything they had to succeed in breaking the curse this Valentine's Eve. And as their vow shimmered out into the universe, it filled both of them with more confidence than they'd ever had that they would succeed.

CHAPTER

TWENTY

On the other side of the world, in the North Pole, Gary turned from staring into the special snow globe they used to see what was going on in the world, and looked up at Santa and Merry. "You can't grant that wish, Santa, no matter how much you want to."

"I know-ho-ho," he said sadly. "Not that it is truly a wish. A vow is a different thing altogether, one that goes to the Eternal Well. But maybe I can wish that the Eternal Well can help them succeed in their vow."

"I think that's a wonderful idea, Nick," Merry said, giving her handsome husband a kiss on the cheek.

Gary tensed for a moment but then sighed thankfully when she didn't start to tear off Santa's clothes, then her own, so she could ride him like he'd never been ridden before. She probably would do that – but later when they were in the privacy of their room and Gary didn't have to see it.

He wasn't certain any amount of elf-soap would remove the stain of that memory from his mind's-eye.

He shook his head and repressed a shudder.

Thankfully everything had returned to how it should because of the sacrifice of those two cupids and the witch with no magic. It was an extra bonus that Santa's wish had worked on Jules in a spectacular way. Her Christmas Spirit had surged out into the world, affecting all the humans and witches she came into contact with with the urge to do some good.

It had even seeped out further than that, affecting those in her neighbourhood in multiple, positive ways. Helped by Bas and Violetta and even Tam – working in the background of course because he couldn't let Jules know he existed let alone was there with Bas in the night working with him to make sure her plans all worked out.

They were all good people and even though they'd caused him a lot of grief recently – unwittingly, sure, but still, a lot of grief, extra work and more inappropriate images than Nick and Merry had furnished him with that he couldn't get out of his mind – for the first time ever, Gary truly wished that they would get what they deserved: a true happy ever after for them all.

"Now that is a wish I can grant," Santa bellowed.

And before Gary could stop him, Santa waved his hand and the tingle of Christmas magic flowed out into the world.

"Oh Nick, what have you done?" Merry groaned.

"Only good things, my dear. Just wait and see."

She looked at Gary like she thought he might help but he just shrugged. "I don't feel anything negative happening in the Aether from him granting my unspoken wish," he said slowly as he sent his magic out into the world and beyond, checking on what his boss had done. "I think maybe he's right. I think maybe this time there will be no consequences from the granting of this wish."

Santa clapped him on the back, sending him stumbling forward. Not that he noticed because he'd turned to give his wife a smacking kiss on the lips. "You two worry-warts. You'll see. There was only good intent in Gary's unspoken wish. And it wasn't about breaking the curse, only seeking happiness for good people who deserve it. Ho-ho-ho, I can't wait to watch what they do with the momentum from his wish. This is going to be good."

Gary and Merry sighed and gave each other a look but then settled down beside Santa to watch the Stevens and their friends work towards the happy ever after they all deserved.

🎄🎅Ho-ho-ho!🎅🎄

Merry Christmas and Seasons Greetings to you all!

There is plenty more to come for the Stevens and their friends. I am going to put them through the wringer - as well as give you (and them) some hot, sexy times plus plenty of mysteries to figure out and evil to overcome.

If you haven't read any of the Gods Cursed Series yet aside from this one and want to dive back into the world of Gods, Goddesses, witches, shifters, demi-Gods, hot sexy times, magic and curses, then you have so much more to read in this series.

Starting with **Love Cursed**, where we find Jules and Bas working against time in the countdown to Valentine's Eve when they can break the curse that plagues them. It's all the fated mates, slow burn, second chance romance with action, magic and a fight against an ancient evil Priestess that you are hanging out for.

And bonus: it's currently available as a free download through the QR code here.

Or you can read the first two chapters here to try it out before you download it for free. After the little sneak peek, you will also find something else pretty special that I am offering just for lovers of the Gods Cursed Series for FREE.

For now though, just turn the page to read the first two chapters of *Love Cursed* ...

LOVE CURSED

GODS CURSED BOOK 1

CHAPTER

ONE

"Would you like a drink, Julianna?"

"Umm ..." Jules blinked rapidly at Simon. Was she supposed to say yes, or no? The information on first dates she'd looked up online hadn't covered this scenario. It was at times like this she really wished she'd inherited her mother's talent for reading minds – although, if she'd inherited her mother's talent, she wouldn't be here. But longing for magic was as useless as longing to have her parents back, so she pushed that thought away as quickly as it had come and tried to read the answer in Simon's eyes.

He began to tap his foot when she didn't answer immediately, then said slowly. "A drink?" His eyes widened a little as he waited for her response.

Did that mean he wanted her to answer yes, or no? Hells, she was so lost.

"Oh, for Goddess-sake! Are you thirsty or not?" the voice in her head snarled.

It was a voice that had come to her on and off all her life, but she'd mostly ignored it. However, something had changed after Christmas and it was now making itself known far more frequently than it ever had before. She had come other think of it as her subconscious rising to the fore as a way to protect herself against increasingly difficult times. She did have a tendency to overthink things and the voice did tend to cut through her overthinking nonsense. She didn't always listen to it, but ...

While it didn't seem particularly happy she was here – it had been very snarky about her date ever since she'd agreed to it – it did have a point right now. Her mouth was incredibly dry, so ... "Yes? Please."

Simon smiled and stood. "Gin and tonic with a twist of lime good for you?"

Yuk. But would he offer that if he didn't think it was the right drink for this situation? Probably not, so ... "Yes please."

A slight nod and another smile.

Another good guess. This was going great even if she did have to drink gin.

"I'll be right back. Make yourself comfortable."

She nodded, even though there was no chance she'd ever be comfortable on this particular sofa. It was over-stuffed, hard and for some strange reason, covered in plastic.

Well, if he truly wanted her comfortable, maybe she didn't have to stay seated.

Jules stood, making a little ripping, sucking sound as the bare part of her legs separated from the plastic – why was it so hot in here? She shouldn't have worn this cream wool dress with its capped sleeves and pretty lace collar. Grandmama always said good wool was cool in summer, warm in winter, but right now, Jules simply found it stifling. However, there was nothing else in her wardrobe that was date worthy.

She quickly sniffed at her armpits, hoping the heat didn't equate to smelly sweat. Thankfully, all she smelled was a faint whiff of her deodorant. Thank the Goddess for that!

Maybe if she walked about a bit, it might help. Waving her hand in front of her face like a fan, she made a little turn around the room. Surely it wasn't rude to look at the artwork and knick-knacks?

She should have done a more thorough job when she'd researched date etiquette. But most of it had been about what date you could first kiss on and what date you could go to second base, who should pay if you went out and so on. Nothing was discussed about a first date where the guy cooked for you at his family home.

It was okay though. She hadn't yet given away that this was the first time she'd been on a date – pitiful given she was 28. Not that she was a virgin – not much better than a virgin, but still, not a virgin. She had some urges and the usual amount of curiosity and it had been easy to assuage that curiosity with a friend at university when she was 20. She couldn't say she had truly enjoyed it, but it had been interesting and she could see that maybe with the right person, it could be pretty special.

Was Simon that someone special? Probably not, but it was something she needed to explore. She owed it to herself to explore it. She truly didn't want to live her life alone. But she hadn't realised how little she knew about dating or being a good date.

Was she being a good date? She was too nervous to know. At least Simon didn't seem to want to chuck her out right away, so that was a good sign. In fact, it seemed like the date was going well.

Date.

Her lips twitched into a smile and, clenching her hands to her chest, she did a little spin on the spot.

She was on a date. An actual date. And her date was making her dinner.

Would he kiss her? She hoped so. Or maybe not. Hells, she didn't know. But it was nice to think there was a chance of something like that happening even if she didn't particularly long for it to happen in the usual tingle-in-the-tummy, curl-the-toes kind of way.

Was that what she would feel if he kissed her? Would it be like kissing that long-ago university friend – something that gave her a little tingle, but more because of the fact it was new rather than creating a great passion. Or would his kiss be more like when Aunt Ophelia kissed her?

The old woman had this thing about kissing on the lips which was a bit odd in a family not given to demonstrative hugging and kissing. But it wasn't even the kissing on the lips that was so bad, it was the fact Aunt O's lips were a curious and shudder-inducing combination of parchment dry yet somehow always sticky. Probably had something to do with the ten-tonne of lipstick she wore. Or the never-ending supply of lollies she munched on.

Thankfully Grandmama had stopped Aunt O from kissing Jules; or touching her as she had a want to do – she was a bit of a close talker – many years ago because her sensitivity to magic had got to the point it was noticeable, and, "*We must never let anyone else know of your affliction before we've found the cure!*" her grandmama had always lectured.

Jules had always hated that lecture and not simply

because it was kind of pointless – it wasn't like she was about to go running around telling everyone about her affliction especially given who her family was and what it could mean if certain people in the community found out. No, she'd hated it because the great Violetta Stevens, Grand Matriarch of the Stevens family and Melbourne Coven Leader, had kept her hope alive for so many years with her talk of a cure.

But there was no cure. No hope. She would always be like this. And if her Grandmama couldn't face the truth of that, well, at least she could, no matter how much it hurt.

And, if she were to look on the bright side, Grandmama's protectiveness and the affliction had saved her from Aunt O's kisses, so, it wasn't all bad.

Although, right now, given nobody but Bas had touched her for years, she almost missed Aunt O's disgusting kisses.

Hells. She did want Simon to kiss her, if only for the aching need inside her to be assuaged. And if anyone could do it, it should be him. She hadn't had any unfortunate reactions to being in this room with him for the ten minutes they had sat chatting – well, he chatted and she listened. He did seem to love talking about his work; and she had to admit it was interesting hearing about the potions he created with the little bit of magic he had access to. Not that he'd put it like that. He'd made it sound like his magic was grand, but she knew better. She wouldn't be here if it was.

But that was by-the-by. Hearing about the kind of magical work he did filled in some gaps she didn't know she had in her knowledge base. The books and grimoires she worked with and catalogued in the Coven Library under Stevens House didn't mention small household spells like the ones he seemed so proud of.

But the best thing was, that even though he spoke about magic, and she'd known coming here that he had access to very little, there didn't seem to be any around him at all. She hadn't even felt a tingle from him when he'd sat on the couch right next to her after taking her cardigan. She also hadn't felt a tingle of anything else looking into his handsome face with his hair slicked back like some mobster from the twenties and a superior smile twitching on his lips as he bragged about his latest stain-removal feat.

Probably not a great sign given this was a date, but beggars couldn't be choosers.

The Council would never countenance her dating anyone outside of the magical community – they didn't know about the university friend – but given her affliction, she couldn't date anyone inside of it, so she'd always been stuck. But after hearing Grandmama complain about him and his family and their ebbing magical abilities and how the rest of the Council were on a mission to oust families that were not pulling their weight, she knew this could be her chance.

She might not want another date with Simon – especially if he kept looking at her as he'd done when she'd arrived, like he was about to win a prize. He had no idea she was no prize despite her family name and their standing in the magical community – but she wasn't about to explain that to him. It certainly wouldn't be a tick in the right column at this early stage.

"Here you go, my dear. Let me know if it's too strong."

She took the proffered drink and sipped obediently, trying very hard not to gag as the horrid taste of juniper and alcohol filled her mouth. Thankfully, he'd made a very weak gin and tonic, so she was able to swallow it and not spray the mouthful all over his beautifully pressed suit. "It's love-ly," she said, smiling up at him.

"You know, gin is what prostitutes used to drink. It was cheap and rotted their brains, so their job was at least bearable."

She widened her smile, trying to ignore the voice in her head. It was particularly acerbic today. When it was like this is was difficult to accept it was her subconscious. Maybe she had multiple personalities. Perhaps her the increasing seriousness of her affliction was also driving her insane.

"You're saner than he is. Do you think he thinks looking at you like that is charming?"

Oh Goddess. Simon *was* looking at her funny. Did she have a maniacal grin on her face? She pressed her lips together and looked away, her gaze lighting on the humongous and ugly portrait that hung over the mantlepiece. "This is ... astonishing."

Simon's gaze immediately swung to the portrait. "Yes, isn't it? We're very proud of it. Mother commissioned the portrait a few years ago and Armando Sinclair himself came to do the drawings. He's a 'normal' but is very talented."

She nodded knowingly even though she had no idea who Armando Sinclair was – obviously someone well-known in stuffy circles going by the expression on Simon's face and his air of general satisfaction as he gestured at the portrait. "It's very ... lifelike. I almost feel like your mother's eyes are following me." She hid a shudder.

"Yes, it's a feature of Armando's work. He likes to draw the viewer into the painting. See how the smile on her face almost says, 'come to me'."

"More like 'run far away, little peasant'."

Jules choked back the urge to laugh as she said to the voice in her mind, *"Not now, please. You can talk as much as you like later. Just not now. I don't want to ruin this. If things go well, I'll have a date on Valentine's Day. I might not ever get another chance."*

An aggravated sigh was her only answer.

"Thank you."

"You won't thank me if you stay much longer with this pillock."

She clapped her hand against her mouth to stop the snort of laughter from erupting.

"Julianna? Are you okay?"

"I'm fine. Drink just went down the wrong way."

He frowned at her. "Perhaps I did make it a little strong. Here, let me fix it."

He took the drink from her – she hoped by some miracle he might not bring it back – then just as he went to turn, a bell sounded from the next room.

"Ah, our dinner is ready. Let me show you to the table and I'll fetch it for us."

She allowed him to take her elbow and lead her into a formal and very stuffy blue and gold dining room – Goddess! Did they think they were living at the Palace at Versailles? – and then stood as he pulled out a chair at one end of the table.

"Sit here and I will be right back with our Pasta al tomato and our Salad al Verde."

"What language does he think he's parroting?"

Jules held onto her snort only as long as it took the door to slap shut behind Simon.

"He's an idiot," the voice said.

"Be nice."

"Hard to in the face of such idiocy. You can't seriously consider going on another date with him?"

"Maybe."

"Well, then, you'd be the idiot. Especially given the fact you have someone so much better waiting in the wings."

Jules snorted. *"If that were true, I wouldn't be here."*

"If only you could see. He's waiting there for both of us. He's—" The voice cut off with a choking sound as pain, sharp and icy, spiked through her head.

"Ow!" she gasped, clutching at her head as the kitchen door swung open and Simon entered with a tray covered with a large and very shiny metal cloche.

"Ta-da. Our dinner is served." Thankfully he was too busy looking at the cloche to notice she was in pain.

She quickly dropped her hands and said, "Yummy," trying her best to cover the fact her eyelid still twitched from the pain echoing through her head. Perhaps she should go and get her head scanned – these attacks were getting worse and worse.

"It won't help," the voice said, the sound of it not much more than a whimper.

"Shut up and go away."

"I beg your pardon?" Simon had stopped a few feet away from the table, his handsome face marred by outraged surprise.

Damn it. Had she said that out loud? "Sorry," she said quickly. "I was talking about my phone. I must have left it on in my handbag in the other room."

"Your phone? I can't hear it ringing."

"Oh, can't you. Well, that's good then. Shall I help you with this?" she said, standing so abruptly she knocked the chair over.

"Careful!" Simon shouted as she made a grab for it, catching it before it hit the floor. "Mama would be extremely annoyed if those chairs were damaged. She hunted for months for just the right shade of blue in the tapestry and just the right honey in the wood and ended up getting them shipped from a monastery high in the Austrian Alps. They are very expensive."

She gingerly put it back in place. "If they are so expensive, should we even eat in here?"

"Of course. Where else would I entertain Julianna Stevens, granddaughter of our Coven Leader?"

"Where else indeed. And please, it's Jules."

"Really?" His tone and the tightening of his mouth suggested what he really meant was 'It's so ... common'. But to his credit, he rallied, and with a nod to her seat, said, "Sit please ... Jules. Let me serve you then we can chat and get to know each other better."

She sat back in the chair very carefully and waited as Simon served the pasta – tomato and basil from the smell. He grated parmesan over it without asking her if she wanted any – she did, but twice the meagre amount he'd put on – placing it down in front of her with a flourish. He then served her a small plate of salad – a few lettuce leaves with a few pieces of tomato and basil and way too much balsamic dressing from the smell and the drenched look of the leaves – and then, after serving himself, took a seat at the other end of the twelve-seater table.

"Bon appetito," he said and tucked in.

"*Idiot,*" the voice muttered, making her snort just as she lifted her first mouthful to her lips. A piece of tomato-soaked pasta dropped from the fork, hit her breast and ran a snail-trail down the front of her cream dress.

"Damn," she muttered.

"Oh, you are a klutz," Simon said. "But here, let me fix that for you. I've been working on a new cleaning spell for just this occasion."

"No, don't—"

But it was too late, he'd released the small spell. It hit her square in the chest, fizzed around her for a moment as if it wasn't going to work and then,

BANG!

Her allergy to magic reacted forcibly. The table in front of her blew up and she was thrown back by the force of the explosion, tomato pasta and salad flying everywhere. She hit the wall with a loud smack of breaking plaster, wood and crockery. Her head hurt from where it had impacted with the wall, but that pulse of pain wasn't as bad as the smarting cuts that sliced her skin everywhere the magic touched her or the nausea roiling in her stomach. She slid down the wall and fell onto her hands and knees, heaving everything she'd eaten in the last half day onto the floor. Somewhere in her mind she was conscious of a voice screaming obscenities.

Despite the pain sparking through her and the fact every movement threatened more vomiting, she managed to look up and across the room.

Simon was trying to extricate himself from a tangle of broken chairs while swearing and screaming like a banshee.

Shit. Had she done that? She had to get over there, apologise, make certain he wasn't so angry he'd do something she really didn't want him to do. Something that would make Grandmama very angry. She pushed groggily to her feet and staggered over to him, somehow managing not to vomit again. "Sorry. So sorry. I didn't mean to ... I can't help it ..." She managed to help him get free of the chairs.

Simon rolled to his side, pushed to his feet and staggered away from her. "That was you?"

"Yes. In part. I'm allergic to magic," she blurted out.

"You ... what? You're magically disabled?"

"Oops. Cat's out of the bag now. Too bad, so sad."

But she barely heard the voice in her head because Simon was looking at her like she was some kind of monster. "A witch who is allergic to magic? Why ... Your family should never let you out of the house! It's criminal. I would never have ... look at what you've done!"

Face hot with her anger and chest heaving, she couldn't stop herself from saying, "It was partly your fault. You shouldn't use magic on others without first asking permission."

"I ... You ..." His mouth opened and closed like a guppy, bits of pasta and tomato falling from his head as he shook his fist at her. "It wouldn't have been a problem if you weren't an abomination. Get out! Get out of my house. I will be seeking reparations from your grandmother, that I promise you. You haven't heard the end of this!"

There were things she should have said to him – he was being very rude when it was half his fault – but what was the point? She wouldn't win him over despite her previous thoughts. And after Grandmama got over her anger, she would cover this up by fixing the damages and wiping memories. She only wished Violetta could wipe her memory because she'd love to forget this disaster. And the dream she'd had that for this once, she wouldn't be alone and loveless on Valentine's Day.

Jules turned, shoulders slumped, arms wrapped around herself. She should have known better than to try for something close to normal.

She grabbed her bag from the other room, limped out the front door and only hoped she wouldn't bump into anyone she knew before she could get home and out of her tomato, basil and blood-soaked dress and have a shower. It was going to be embarrassing enough having to explain this to her grandmama without having to deal with anyone else seeing her as well.

And Bas wouldn't be pleased.

She sighed. She'd have to avoid him until morning when he was back in his cat form. Pity. She could do with one of his hugs right about now but that would have to wait until tomorrow night when he was in his human form again and she'd made certain he wouldn't go after Simon.

Her lip wobbled and she swiped at the tears that fell down her cheeks. Why did her life have to be so complicated and difficult?

Thankfully, the voice remained silent. Good. She really couldn't deal with it right now.

CHAPTER

TWO

"Bastien? Where are you?"

"Shh." He poked his head out of his room to wave Tamuel, his cupid 'brother', in from the hallway. Despite being blind in his human form, he could still see the cupid's aura shining in the darkness of the hallway due to the enormous power he held, jewel bright with greens and purples and yellows and vibrating outwards. "Tighten your hold on your powers. Jules is asleep in the room next door."

"At this hour?"

"She went to bed early with a headache. I don't want to wake her."

"No. I imagine you don't."

He nodded at his old friend. There was no way Jules could know what they were up to. Too much was at stake if they wanted this to work.

And he needed it to work. He'd lived without hope for so long. The unbinding of the curse that had made his life a living hell for 2,000 years had seemed nothing but a pipe dream for so long.

A pipe dream tied to a small loophole once every 200 years on Valentine's Day Eve.

A loophole that had seemed beyond his grasp when one after another reincarnation of Julianna Stevius – Lianna to everyone who had known her back then – barely acknowledged he was alive, let alone had the curiosity to question the nightmares they endured and the fact they reacted badly to magic. They'd just ... accepted, Lianna's spirit pushed so far down inside them by the curse that he could do nothing about the silent screaming he sometimes thought he heard from her.

But Jules was different from all who came before, and her birth and the fact Tamuel had finally found the journal had—

"Where do you want me to drop the boxes?" Tamuel asked.

"In the library—no! Don't use your magic here. You'll hurt Jules – I can't believe you'd forget."

"I didn't forget. But she's not in this room – you never said she had become *that* sensitive."

Bastien shrugged. Violetta could barely even touch her granddaughter now for fear of Jules' magical sensitivity reacting to the power just under her skin. He never thought he'd be grateful the curse had taken all but a smidgeon of his power – and in the last year or so, it had taken nearly all of what he had left – but at least it allowed him to touch her. She was rarely ever touched by anyone anymore. "I thought I'd mentioned to you that it's been getting worse lately. Much worse."

"A sign?"

He shrugged again. Tamuel's guess was as good as his. "We also don't want Violetta sensing you were here when she gets back. She's not expecting you to arrive with the shipment of ancient books and manuscripts until next week – you're supposed to be stuck in Rome." Tamuel's well-constructed role of magical artefacts dealer, Tomaso di Erosi, alongside a friendship he'd struck up with Violetta and her deceased husband many years ago, had helped as a cover for why he was around so much, but it wouldn't explain why he was here now at this hour or why he had the journal they needed Jules to 'find'.

"Here – take my arm. I'll lead you downstairs," Tamuel said.

Bastien brushed his friend's arm aside, trying very hard not to be annoyed, but the cupid should know better than to treat him like an invalid. Especially after all this time. But sometimes he slipped. Bastien put it down to his cupid need to please – and that was the only reason he held his temper as he said, "I might be blind in this form, but I know my way around this house and the library better than you – I have lived here ever since Tamara Stevens built it 150 years ago."

"Of course. Sorry. You are right. Lead the way."

He made his way out into the hall, down the stairs, across the foyer to the door that led to the library that lay in the secret underground caverns deep below Stevens House. He led Tamuel down the four flights of stairs, their foot-steps echoing off the stone walls and arched ceiling. The sound changed as they stepped into the huge library at the end of the stairs, disappearing in the high arches of wood and stone overhead and the stacks that filled the cavernous space and multiple specialised rooms that made up the library.

He didn't bother to turn on the lights in the massive chandeliers overhead. He certainly didn't need the light to get around and Tamuel had the eyesight of a cupid so didn't even need to use his magic to light his way.

As he moved into the library, there came a rustling from the far corners and a rushing pressure – the ghosts of Stevens House coming out to protect what was theirs from intruders. "It's just me and Tamuel," he said. They immediately settled down and went back to whatever they did when they weren't haunting someone or protecting the library.

"So it's safe to teleport the boxes in now?" Tamuel said, pulling Bastien's attention back to the job at hand.

"Yes. There's enough stone and dirt between us. Jules won't be affected. And any leftover magic will be syphoned into the magical ark that Violetta created recently to protect Jules from the latent magic in many of the books, so she can continue to work down here. So neither of them will sense you used any magic down here even if they came down in half an hour."

"Clever." There was a light thump as the load of boxes filled with old books, journals and manuscripts landed at the base of the steps. Good. Jules wouldn't miss them there. "What now?"

"Unpack half of the top box and put the books on the kitchen table in a pile with the journal on the top."

"The kitchen table?"

Bastien nodded. "Jules won't be able to ignore them. And when she sees the age of the journal, she won't be able to stop herself from reading it before she does anything else."

"Are you certain?"

Bastien raised his brow. "Does a cat love cream?"

"I don't know – do you?"

"Ha." He didn't bother mentioning that when forced into his cat body during the day, he no longer touched dairy – it made him feel a little ill now like it would a real cat. Not a good sign at all.

"Here, hold the journal while I take care of the rest."

Tamuel pushed an old leather-bound manuscript into his hands – Jules would be horrified neither of them were wearing cotton gloves to handle it. Even so, his fingers tightened around the soft leather binding. "Hello, old friend."

He couldn't believe he was finally holding it. It had taken so long to track it down, and when Tamuel had told him this last Christmas that he had a lead he knew would allow them to find it, Bas had tried to stop his expectations from soaring – they'd had so many leads that had gone nowhere over the years. But still he'd hoped more than he'd ever hoped before because this had truly felt like their last chance.

And now he was holding it in his hands.

He'd spent many hours watching Esta write this journal, listening to her ponder what to put into it about the curse and what had happened to him and Lianna. It was meant to be a bridge between him and the Stevius family after she'd gone, to explain the curse – a curse that cruelly stopped him from talking about it and what had happened – and to ask for help in finding a way to break it.

But this journal was more than that. It was a history of his and Lianna's love.

Esta had written about how he and Lianna had met, how it had been love at first sight, how, despite Lianna's vows and his job as a cupid, neither of them had been able to do anything but give in to their desires. With one meeting of gazes in that crowded marketplace, he'd known she was his soulmate and they were destined for each other.

A fact that had made him the happiest cupid alive.

Until Clodia had used it against them to curse them.

If not for Esta, he would have lost himself to madness. But Esta had come back in secret after the dust had settled and found him, taking him to her family. Even so young, she'd had the power to bind him to her sister to keep him safe. The only thing she couldn't tell him was what had happened to his son. She went back to serve out her time with the Vestal Virgins, always on the lookout for information about the baby, but never found anything.

He assumed the baby was either found by someone – maybe Eros given the baby would have been born a cupid and he would have been drawn to it by the cupid powers – or had died in the explosion of power, his soul and body mercifully taken to the heavens. Eros of course had studiously ignored him since he was cursed so he could never find out if his father had indeed taken his grandson under his wing. In regard to the latter ... well, he tried very hard not to think about it, but of late it had snuck in more and more often as the most probable explanation for what had happened to the newborn baby.

Either way, the loss of his son was an eternal grief, one that the years had only dulled not made disappear.

Maybe now he had the diary and breaking the curse was closer than it had ever been, he'd be able to find out. But first, they had to break the curse.

His fingers curled around the journal even more tightly. They had so much riding on it. And if it did what they hoped it would, he would finally be able to truly pay Esta back for all she'd done for him.

Years after that horrible night of death and loss, when

Esta had finally been released from her 30 years of service, he'd thanked her for all she'd done by vowing to always be a guardian to her and her family. Not a selfless vow given he wanted to be close when Lianna was reborn into her family line as all witches were every few hundred years.

Unfortunately, knowledge of why he was cursed, and how he came to be bonded to the Stevius family, died with Esta's great-great-granddaughter when the journal he now held in his hand was lost in a house fire – or so he'd thought. Hope had died, little by little with every century that passed and nobody questioned what forced him to live as a cat by day, blind man by night or why he was struck down with extreme pain if he ever tried to talk about any of it. Pain that only got worse if he ever tried to be more than a guardian towards Lianna's reincarnations.

Life had become monotonous and hopeless until Tamuel found him a century ago and told him he wanted to help. He would never have thought a fellow cupid had it in them to care about anything other than their job, but Tamuel had proved to be different.

He'd said that all curses were a horrifying cruelty, a wrong that needed to be righted if they could. Not only that, but he'd also had much to say about how wrong it was that Eros had never tried to break the curse binding his son – and one of the greatest cupids of his time – keeping him from his soulmate. He also thought it was his job, as a cupid, to put two lovers back together who should never have been parted.

It had given Bastien hope; hope that had grown with Jules' birth. It was like Lianna was more alive in her than ever before. And somehow, he was more than a guardian to her. They were best friends.

It would be different this time. It had to be.

He took in a deep breath. "This is going to work," he said to Tamuel.

Tamuel put his arm around Bastien's shoulder. "Yes, it is. I'm certain of it. It's long past time this curse was ended."

Bastien swallowed hard. "Yes, it is."

Tamuel squeezed his shoulder and then turned back to his task. A few moments later, he asked, "Does it matter where on the table I put these?"

"No. Anywhere will get her attention. She has this thing about books and food—" He whipped around at a sound coming from upstairs, his hand going out to slap against Tamuel's chest. "Did you hear that?"

"What?"

There was another shuffling thunk and a curse. "That. Jules. She's moving around upstairs."

"How can you tell it's her? I can barely hear anything."

"She just swore under her breath."

"You really do have the hearing of a cat."

"Can you finish up down here without me?"

"I think I can manage such a difficult task by myself," Tamuel said.

Bastien ignored the sarcasm and ran to the stairs.

"Wait!" Tamuel called out.

He stopped. "Shh. She'll hear you."

"Sorry."

"Well? What did you stop me for?" He really needed to get upstairs. Jules sounded like she was limping. And was that blood he could smell? And tomatoes? What the hell?

"The journal." The flaring movement of the cupid's aura showed Bastien that Tamuel held out his hand, pointing to the book clutched against Bastien's chest.

He couldn't believe he'd forgotten he held it. It would

have been a disaster if Jules had seen it in his arms. The curse would never let him hand over such essential information to her so easily. As it was, even helping Tamuel to set up the journal for Jules to find caused a burning sensation in his chest that wasn't exactly pleasant. "Here." He put the journal down on top of the boxes Tamuel had magicked in minutes ago then took the stairs two at a time.

He burst out of the stairwell into the foyer and stopped.

Jules wasn't in the foyer – there was no sign of her blue and green aura with its dark heart of amethyst glowing in the cavernous space. But she was close. Her presence called to him like a beacon, especially when something was wrong.

And there definitely was something wrong.

I HOPE you enjoyed that little snippet of **Love Cursed**. If you would like to read more, you can download your copy here:

Before you go, I have something a little extra special (slow burn, friends to lovers, deadly secrets and more) for you right here - a FREE prequel novel for the Gods Cursed Series featuring Tam and his secret love, Korinna, at the training camp where they met.

Just turn the page to find out how you can get your FREE copy of *Fractured Curse* ...

LOVE A FREE BOOK?

YOUR FREE BOOK IS WAITING

GET YOUR EXCLUSIVE PREQUEL TO THE GODS CURSED SERIES RIGHT HERE:

Cursed to never be loved; fated to never be alone ...

Cursed cupid Tamuel has been told he will never love or be loved, a fate to which he's long been resigned. Yet from the moment he meets powerful trainee witch Korinna Soteira at the Amazonian and Gargarean training camp, he knows this to be a lie – he loves Korinna like he's loved nothing and no-one in his life. But his curse is right in one respect: he may be able to love, but he can never *be* loved. Korinna will only ever be his friend, a fact he has spent the last twenty years coming to terms with.

However, malignant forces are stirring in the darkest reaches of the Realms. They have plans to use Korinna and her unusual powers – plans that can only be thwarted by the cursed cupid and an impossible love. Yet breaking

Tamuel's curse now could release a force too ancient to destroy – and thus destroy any future.

What if the only way to survive the present is to place the future in peril?

Fractured Curse is a prequel novella to my popular Gods Cursed Series centring on unknown history between two of readers' favourite characters from the series. It takes place 2000 years before the events in ***Love Cursed*** and can be read as an introduction into the world or at any time during the reading of the series.

It's exclusive to my newsletter subscribers, so to get your copy, just follow the QR code or link below, fill in your details and it will be winging its way to you along with other free reads, deals and bookish info.

Get My Free Copy of Fractured Curse Here:
https://www.subscribepage.com/fracturedcurse_signup

JOIN LEISL'S LEGENDS

Subscribe to (or follow) me (via the QR code) at my Leisl's Legends page on REAM—a new subscription app like Patreon except it's designed especially for readers and authors for an amazing reading experience— and you will get early access to  *The Huntress and the Vampire King*, my hot enemies to lovers, witch-and-vampire-licious urban fantasy romance that readers over there are already in love with. It's the prequel novel to the first book in the Blood-Rites Series - *The Blood of the Seer*. Be the first to find out where it all began with Anita and Hei's love story.

You will also get exclusive early access to the next book

in the **Gods Cursed Series** and can comment on the story as I write it! Your feedback could be essential in shaping the next book in the series.

Be part of creating the stories you love AND get exclusive access to a whole range of goodies including other WIPs, bonus content, voting rights, signed books and much, much more.

BECOME A LEGEND NOW!
https://reamstories.com/leislleightonauthor

THE HUNTRESS AND THE VAMPIRE KING

She hates the vampire who saved her; he holds the key to her fate ...

Hunter-witch Anita Middleton wants revenge against the violent vampire cults that murdered her father and has worked hard to become one of the best vampire hunters there is. But on a difficult hunt she is caught in an ambush and is mortally wounded ... only to be saved by a mysterious warrior. A warrior with brilliant blue eyes and long silver-blonde hair who fights with a grace and violence like nothing she's seen. It is only after she wakes in the heart of his palazzo that she realises her saviour is a vampire - and according to her brother and mentor, this vampire king is their ally.

Lord Hei rules over an empire of witches, humans and vampires who have been trying to keep the vicious vampire cults, the Wild and Dark Brethren, at bay for centuries. Then he saves Anita and knows with one look she is the prophecied Huntress who could be his downfall or his salvation - and she is also his fated mate. But she struggles to trust him as her hatred of vampires is deep-seated. And she *needs* to trust him because only he can offer the specialised training a Huntress needs so her power won't overwhelm her.

But with the Dark Brethren mysteriously amassing, he has little time to win her over. And Anita must go on a crash course to learn how to control her Huntress magic ... or go slowly and violently insane.

The Huntress and the Vampire King is the exciting action-packed prequel novel to **The Blood of the Seer**.

If you love your vampires hot with a bit of The Witcher thrown in and your heroines as kick-arse as Buffy and even more tortured, if you love fated mates, enemies to lovers, chosen ones and epically hot  **romance mixed with action and mystery, then *The Huntress and the Vampire King* is what you've been waiting for.**

Sign up to Leisl's Legends (via the QR code above) and start reading exclusive early release chapters of it now!

BECOME A LEGEND NOW!
https://reamstories.com/leislleightonauthor

ALSO BY LEISL LEIGHTON

GODS CURSED SERIES

A Love Cursed Christmas Wish

Love Cursed

Soul Cursed

Blood Cursed

Hearts Cursed

Fates Cursed

Witch Cursed

Dragon Cursed

(Coming 2026)

BLOOD-RITES SERIES

The Blood of the Seer

The Blood of the Sire

The Blood of the Son

(Coming 2027)

BLOOD-RITES PREQUEL AND BONUS MATERIAL

The Huntress and the Vampire King

The Middleton Manifesto

(Available now via Leisl's Legends subscription)

PACK BOUND SERIES

Pack Bound

Moon Bound

Shifter Bound

Wolf Bound

Witch Bound

(A Pack Bound Series Prequel Novella)

BOX SET

Pack Bound Series Collection Books 1-4

DAWN OF THE CURSE

A PACK BOUND PREQUEL SERIES

Soul Bound

Alpha Bound

Hunter Bound

Fae Bound

(Coming in 2027)

~

ANTHOLOGIES

A Perfectly Paranormal Valentine

A Perfectly Paranormal Halloween

A Perfectly Paranormal Easter

A Perfectly Paranormal Christmas

A Perfectly Paranormal Prophecy

(Coming in 2027)

~

As well as writing sexy, epic and romantic paranormal novels, I write mysterious and emotional romantic suspense novels too. Check out the following titles for amazing, suspenseful reads:

Storm Haven Series

Need You Tonight

The Devil Inside

~

CoalCliff Stud Series

Climbing Fear: Book 1

Blazing Fear: Book 2

~

Echo Springs Series

Dangerous Echoes: Book 1

Books 2-4 in this series, (written by Daniel deLorne, TJ Hamilton and Shannon Curtis) are also available now at all ebook retailers.

ABOUT LEISL

Leisl Leighton is a tall red head with an overly large imagination. As a child, she identified strongly with Anne of Green Gables, and like Anne, is a voracious reader and born performer.

It came as no surprise when she went on to a career as a performer, script writer, script doctor, stage manager and musical director for cabaret and theatre restaurants.

After starting a family, Leisl stopped performing and began writing the stories plaguing her dreams. She now writes emotional stories mixed with mystery and a little bit of what goes bump in the night.

Her novels have won and placed in writing contests here and overseas. She is a passionate advocate for the romance genre, was President of Romance Writers of Australia from 2014-2017 and when she's not writing romantic stories of redemption, she is helping other authors reach their dreams with her Author Services. You can contact Leisl through her website via the QR Code above or here: https://www.leislleighton.com

those days usually are meant to fill the participant with the same kind of spirit that Christmas is about, so I feel that everyone has an inkling of what I am talking about.

I do know that many people suffer hardship and loneliness at this time of the year and so don't feel about the season the way I do. But I hope those people at some stage in their lives experience the joy and happiness that encompasses the Christmas Spirit and that it helps to lift them up in times of darkness and helps get them through.

That is my wish to everyone this Christmas season - that everyone in the world will get to experience the essence of the Christmas Spirit during the next year. That they will appreciate family and friends; that they are successful in some endeavour; that they can find joy in helping someone else in some way; that they get to experience love in some form; and that they want this for others too.

For me, I am blessed to have so many people, both family and friends, around me that support me and share the ups and down with. They fill me with love and the encouragement I needed to keep pushing on even in times of hardship, grief and darkness - and this year has been full of those things. It is because of them that I am filled with thankfulness and Christmas Spirit at this time of year.

Thanks to all of you - you are superstars!

Of course, special thanks have to go out to my hubby, Mark, and my two beautiful boys, Jacob and Nathaniel, and to my parents, Kerrie and Jim, whose support has never wavered and whose love I could never do without. Love you all.

Aside from great family and friends, a writer needs a Coven of writing peeps all their own. Thanks need to go to these special people for encouraging me in this endeavour and giving me the strength to push on through all the highs and lows of doing this crazy writing thing—Anita and Marnie (my writing retreat buddies), Samantha and Helen (my fellow lovers of sparkly unicorns), Laura, Chris and finally Frana. I couldn't have gotten here without you.

Thanks once again to the insanely talented Samantha Marshall for her brilliant covers. Every day I thank the universe for bringing us together and for being able to count you friend.

Thanks also to Kerril Romanis for using her exceptional skills and editing my book at the last moment when other editing options feel through.

Thoughts and thanks also to my bestie, Helen, who is always with me and forever in my thoughts, and to the first writing friend I ever had, Liz. And this year, I must add my dearest Aunty Sue to that list of those dear to me who have been taken too soon. A part of all of them will always live on in my writing because I would never have got published without their helpful feedback and constant cheering support. Helen, Liz and Aunty Sue - you will always be a part of my stories.

And a big shout out to all my friends in Romance Writers of Australia—you are inspiration and mentor rolled into a big ball of supportive writerly love. Thank you.

The final person I have to thank is my agent, Alex Adsett, for believing in me and my work and always backing every decision I make. Your confidence in me helps me believe I can actually do this writing thing no matter the path I take. Eternal thanks.

Happy Christmas and Seasons Greetings to you all. I hope all of your Christmas Wishes can come true.

Leisl Leighton 🌲 🤍